Calling Juliet Bravo

Calling Juliet Bravo

New Arrivals

by Mollie Hardwick

from the TV series
Created by IAN KENNEDY MARTIN

British Broadcasting Corporation

Published by the
British Broadcasting Corporation
35 Marylebone High Street
London W1M 4AA

ISBN 0 563 17961 9

First published 1981

Printed in England by
Love & Malcomson Ltd.,
Brighton Road, Redhill, Surrey.

Contents

1 Only Lookin'

Inspector Jean Darblay parked her red Mini expertly in the private car-park adjoining Hartley Police Station, more familiarly known as The Nick. Basically an ugly Victorian building, it had acquired, since Jean had been in charge of the Hartley section, the air of an establishment trying hard to live up to a lady who ruled with a firm hand, suffering neither fools nor disorder gladly. In the time since her appointment she had broken down a lot of the original resentment felt against her by the men under her command. They were, of course, still male chauvinists — what else would they be, reared in the industrial north of England? But they couldn't help but respect their woman boss's firmness and fairness and clear-sightedness. She didn't pretend to be an imitation man, just a woman who did her job very well.

As she locked the car door and hooked her bag on to her shoulder she was aware, out of the corner of her eye, of a man standing in the street, at the edge of the car-park, watching her. Another of Hartley's growing number of unemployed. The little valley town crouching on the edge of Pendle Forest and the Pennines had once been alive with the hum of mills, its old cobbled streets ringing under the feet of workers. Now it was the ghost of its old self, the dwelling-place of the poor and the alien, a breeding-place for petty crime. To be a policeman in Hartley was no job for anybody who wanted either a life without incident or one of feverish excitement. Robberies, protest rallies and marches, grievous bodily harm and common assault, juvenile delinquency and battered wives, stolen cars and mugged old people: these made up the normal pattern of life at Hartley Nick.

Jean greeted the Sergeant on the desk, George Parrish, a

mild unfussed man who had been friendly to Jean in the days when his colleague Joe Beck had fought her with weapons varying from heavy patronage to barely veiled rudeness.

'Morning, Ma'am.'

'Any problems?'

'Not so far. Message from the Super on your desk.'

'Right. What's the matter with the heating? Somebody think we've turned into Eskimos overnight?'

Parrish grinned. 'It's the boiler again. I'll have it looked at.'

'Have it ripped out, more like. That sort of gadget went out with oil lamps.' She passed into her office, neat and sparsely-furnished, but with feminine touches about it; a photograph on the desk of Tom, her husband, beaming under his mop of curly dark hair, a vase on the window-sill filled with flowers from their garden. To Jean her home was a refuge, the place they had chosen together and worked on, Tom exercising his skills of carpentry and design (he had been a design engineer with British Leyland before losing his job by closure) in the hours when he wasn't working as a Social Services officer. It was work he had, rather surprisingly, chosen to do – out of character, people had said. Jean had backed him up all along the line, even when their ways crossed, aware that the rewards balanced poorly against the failures and disappointments. Let him do the work as long as he could, then, perhaps, find a job where he could use his professional qualifications.

Sergeant Beck entered, looming large, his broad give-nothing-away face set in its usual impassive lines. Once Jean's worst enemy, he had come round, to his own surprise, to admiring her. At first he'd missed his ales with Inspector Denton, her predecessor, but Jean was no ladylike sipper of effete pink beverages – she drank her ale when occasion arose for being sociable, just enough to make a man feel relaxed and comfortable, never overdoing it. Beck hadn't a lot of time for women, by and large. He had divorced his own wife four years before. It was an open wound in his mind that she had been given custody of their daughter, Carol, the child he adored, the person closest to him in all the world.

Carol was ten now. He saw her on average four times a year, going over for the purpose to Northern Ireland, where Marcia was now living with her parents. Bloody Ireland: couldn't she have settled somewhere a bit nearer? Only a woman would have picked on it. Bloody women.

But Carol would be a woman one day, not his beloved child any more. He hoped – and Beck was not given to undue optimism – that she'd turn out something like Inspector Darblay. It would be hard to guess from his manner to his superior that he felt like this, but Jean expected neither smiles nor compliments. All she asked was co-operation and goodwill; and from Beck she was now getting both.

She had had no trouble with Detective Constable Roland Bentley, just twenty, *naïf*, inclined to find himself on the receiving end of dirty work; except for a brief rebellion about having to make the coffee. Bentley, whose hair, springing up from his high brow, was so short that he looked at first glance like a skinhead, more often than not found himself driving endless miles (car-sick as he tended to be on the moors) in pursuit of suspects, or legging it breathlessly through the streets after flying forms. Sometimes he had dreams of doing something else. Jean was mildly fond of him, but she wouldn't have bet heavily on his enduring career and promotion in the Force.

Together she and Beck discussed the predictable business of the day. Then there was a visit from Chief Inspector Jack Wigan, in charge of Hartley's CID. They had crossed swords in the early days, when the staid, conservative Wigan had found it hard to take that she, though not his boss, was above him in rank. But time, and a certain conscious exertion of charm on her part, had largely won him over. There had been a very successful dinner-party at the Darblays', on the night when the conjurer had been stabbed by his girl-friend, down at the the little Victoria and Albert theatre; since then he had looked upon Jean in his own mind as a woman who could cook, which made him feel better about her as a woman in authority. This morning he was in a good mood, trotting out his stock jokes. He stayed and chatted, ignoring Jean's glances at her watch.

At lunchtime she and Beck went over to the pub. The man who had been watching her early that morning was still there, standing purposelessly a few yards away from where he had been before. This time she took notice of his appearance: shortish, utterly undistinguished, colourless, National Health glasses, shabby coat, hands in pockets. She directed Beck's attention to him.

'Know that one, Joseph?'

'Can't say I do, Ma'am. Just another no-hoper, would you say?'

'Probably. Only he's been there all morning. Unless he's been off and come back. Seems to be watching whoever goes in and out.'

'Thinking of joining the Force,' said Beck with heavy humour.

'I doubt it.' Over lunch, Jean forgot about the lingering man. They came back to the Nick in the company of Detective Sergeant Melchett of CID, talking, so that if the watcher *was* anywhere about she failed to notice him.

But when she left, early in the evening, he was there again, still and silent in the light from a street-lamp. Jean stopped, then went back inside. Beck was on the desk.

'Joseph, I want you to go and sort out that character who's hanging around near my car. The same man we saw at lunchtime.'

'Sort him out, Ma'am?'

'Tell him to buzz off, or words to that effect. Tell him he'll be had for loitering with intent if he keeps on at it.'

'Loitering with what intent, would you say?'

'How do I know? Nicking cars, nicking things out of them. Just tell him to make himself scarce, if he doesn't want his collar felt.'

'Yes, Ma'am.' Privately Beck thought she was making a fuss about nothing. But women had funny instincts for trouble, he'd allow them that.

When he returned, she looked sharply up from the *Police Gazette*.

'Well?'

'I asked him his business, and he said "Only lookin'"' That was all I could get out of him. A nut, I reckon.'

'Maybe. Has he gone?'

'Yes.'

'Good. 'Night, Joseph.'

Beck watched her go, a slim brisk figure in the berry-red coat that covered her uniform, the lamp above the door reflecting in her shining cap of brown hair.

At supper, Tom was mildly amused at her mention of the incident.

'Why didn't you sort him out yourself, then?'

'Oh, I don't know. Next time I will – if there is a next time. I just thought somebody like that would take more notice of a man. You know what they are.'

'It's not like you to bother about such details. Anyway, the odds are he isn't a nut, in the sense you mean. More likely to be an inadequate type, no job, no background, looking for reassurance in the strong arm of the law. Something like that.'

'Don't you give me that Social Services psychological rubbish, Tom Darblay! If we were all sorry for everybody, like you, the courts would go out of business and we might as well . . .'

The telephone rang.

'Oh, blast. Answer that, will you?' Tom looked pained, his fork half-way to his mouth, 'All right, *I* will. Just cover my plate.'

At first, after the pay-phone pips, there seemed to be nobody at the other end of the telephone. In the silence that followed Jean's curt statement of the number she glared at the instrument. Not another heavy breather, for Heaven's sake! But at last a voice said hesitantly 'Inspector?'

'This is Mrs Darblay.' Jean preferred to keep her public and private lives separate. 'Who's that speaking?'

The voice was thin, Hartley-accented. 'It's me . . .'

'Who's me?'

Another silence. 'I only wanted a word with yer . . .'

'Well, you're having it. What's the trouble?'

There was a sound that might have been a sigh, then the telephone was put down.

'Who was that?' Tom asked.

'I've no idea. Not a heavy breather, anyway. How do they get hold of our number? I've a good mind to have it changed or go ex-directory.' She was curiously unwilling to discuss with Tom the quavering voice, and the uneasy feeling somewhere about the small of her back that usually meant an intuitive foreknowledge of trouble.

The three days that followed were uneventful, so much so that Parrish suggested to Bentley that the villains had gone off in a body for a mid-winter away-break. Bentley replied that he for one was only too glad of a bit of desk work in the warm. Jean, hurrying to and from her car through the cold muggy air that was Hartley's speciality, saw no sign of the lurker and was thankful. Rare interludes of peace, like this, were too good to be interrupted by trivial nuisances. The man was obviously not surreptitiously removing car-parts, which was about the only damage he looked capable of doing.

When the telephone rang that night she answered it prepared to dismiss the caller crisply. But it was young Constable Moss from the Nick.

'Sorry to disturb you, Ma'am. You're wanted down at Alma Street – number 29a.'

'What is it – assault?'

'Seems to be rape.'

'Oh. Right, I'll be there in ten minutes. Who answered the call?'

'Sergeant Beck and Constable Bentley, Ma'am.' She detected concern in Moss's voice, and knew that he was thinking of his young wife and their baby, alone in the isolated house on the hill in Three Area. He hated night-shifts that took him away from home and Sheila. He would like to change his job – if he didn't enjoy it so much . . .

Number 29a was a basement flat in a terrace of run-down Victorian houses. Jean made her way down the short flight of stone steps, past the lighted window. Sounds and voices were coming from inside.

The room was low-ceilinged, furnished with what were obviously landlady's throw-outs, a few cheap modern chain-store prints on the walls – leering moppets with big eyes embracing cute puppies, Degas ballet-dancers and a lurid landscape of an Italian lake. Beck and Bentley sat at the table, Beck looking huge in the small room, Bentley scribbling in his note-book. On a chair by the dishevelled divan a girl sat rocking to and fro in the time-old way of distressed women. A pink dressing-gown was round her shoulders, her long straight hair fell forward over her face, and she was sobbing, loud rhythmic hoarse sobs.

Bentley looked up with relief as Jean entered.

'Well?' she said.

'I haven't got a lot down, Ma'am. It's – not very easy.' He nodded towards the girl.

'How much?'

He consulted his notes. 'It seems to have happened about an hour ago. A man walked in, nobody she knew, assaulted her and ran off. She got upstairs to the pay-phone on the landing and called us. Since then she's not made a lot of sense.'

'I see.' She gestured to them to remove themselves to the far end of the room, and sat down beside the girl.

'Like to tell me anything? You didn't know the man?'

The drooping head was shaken.

'Was the door locked? No? That was a bit careless, wasn't it?' It was clear to Jean that not much was to be got out of the distraught victim at that moment. She told Beck to call an ambulance, and herself went in it with the girl, leaving Beck and Bentley to take full notes and lock up the flat.

The police doctor pronounced Shirley Coates to be in need of sedation and hospital treatment. In the curtained cubicle of Hartley General, Jean sat by Shirley's side until the sedative had taken effect, telling the nurse to call her when the patient recovered consciousness.

In the early morning of the next day she was there again, listening to the whispered, fragmentary story. Shirley was a student, in digs for the first time in her life. She had no boyfriends in the district, only a steady one at home.

13

Jean read between the lines that Shirley thought the shoddy flatlet romantic and enjoyed the freedom of being on her own away from her family. Yes, she had noticed that people looked in through the top half of the window visible from the street; no, she didn't bother much about drawing the curtains except at night – they were a bad fit anyway.

'And you're quite sure you didn't know the man? What did he look like?'

'I told the policeman.'

'Yes, but tell me.'

'Well . . . nothing special. Sort of thirtyish, thin. Not very clean.' She shuddered. 'I don't want to talk about him. I don't want to know about men, ever again.'

Jean patted the clenched hand and called the nurse. It was a genuine case, forensic evidence had established that, not one of the common hysterical attempts women made to draw attention to themselves. No recognition of the man, so no revenge motive. Just a brutal assault on an ignorant, fatally careless girl who would probably suffer repercussions from the shock for years, if not all her life.

Back at the Nick she called a parade. 'I want that Alma Street case gone into properly, and I want the man caught. The girl didn't know him, but somebody else will. There's always plenty of people with nothing to do but sit at the window, watching what goes on in the street. Find out if there's ever been trouble in that flat before.'

'I hope I'm the one to get him,' Moss said to Bentley. 'No woman's safe while there's villains like that around. I know what I'd have happen to 'em, and it wouldn't be just a cautioning . . .'

As the day went by, the memory of Shirley Coates's distress faded from Jean's mind. When action had been taken in a case, one had to switch if off and switch on to the next one. Only a shadow of it stayed with her when the time came to telephone Tom to say that she would be home early, ahead of him.

She drew up outside the house in the quiet road, thankful to be home, and went to unlock the garage. As she came back to the car a figure rose from behind the hedge, only a foot or two away from her. Startled, she gave an involuntary cry and jumped back. It was the lurker, drab, pale, spectacled, an incongruous sight so near her home. Within an instant she had collected herself, and was speaking into her personal radio.

'Juliet Bravo to Hartley. Man lurking possibly with intent outside . . .'

He interrupted her, in the flat voice that had come over the telephone.

'I've done nowt wrong, missis. I were only lookin'.'

'Get out!' she said, surprised by her own savagery. 'Go on, out of it. Any more of this and you'll be inside. Get on, now!'

A flurry of footsteps and he was gone.

Tom said, 'It's ridiculous. You, versus some dirty-macintosh type that runs when you bark at him. What're you worrying about?'

'Nothing. I just don't like nuisances turning up here, that's all. He's not a flasher, he's nothing. And don't tell me I ought to have asked him in for a cosy evening round the fire.'

'We could have run to it – I bought an extra chop,' Tom said, but the joke misfired.

To Parrish she said next morning 'I want my calls monitored, George. Anybody who doesn't sound as if they know me, ask them their name and business. I don't want oddments under my feet.'

Parrish glanced at her curiously, wondering what was biting her. The call that came mid-morning, hesitantly asking for her, ceased when he questioned the caller, and he said nothing about it to her. A message came through from Hartley General that Shirley Coates had been discharged and taken home by her mother. Nothing had been discovered about her attacker. The *Hartley Clarion*, hungry for news, made much of the story, writing up the Alma Street Rapist into a horror-figure worthy of national headlines, and Shirley's former landlady equally enjoyed the importance of giving interviews ('I warned Rape Victim of Danger to Lonely Girls') and attacks by neighbours who blamed her for not warning Shirley more sharply. It seemed that there were two sides to being famous.

Saturday morning: a beautiful Saturday off. Daringly, Jean telephoned the hairdresser and made an appointment for an eleven o'clock shampoo and set. Usually it was impossible for her to book appointments with any certainty of keeping them, and she was used to washing her hair at home and blow-drying it, neither as pleasant nor as satisfactory as sitting in a salon being pampered. Perhaps Mr Xavier's manicurist would be free, too. She lifted the telephone again.

The doorbell rang. Jean glanced at her watch. It was about the time the parcel post came; Tom was expecting some books. As a matter of routine she always looked through the Judas-hole in the door to identify the caller. Just for once she went straight to the door and opened it, her smile ready for the postman, with his eccentrically courteous 'Good morning, dear madam.'

The man was in the hall before she had even registered who it was, kicking the door shut behind him. He grabbed her, unprotected by her uniform, dressed in her casual zipped breakfast-gown, and forced her against the wall with a hard hurting grip, knocking the breath out of her, a bony knee pressed into her body, onion-laden breath in her face.

She was very frightened, more frightened than she had ever been in her life before, and there had been some tight spots. Panic rose in her throat. Tom was in town tying up a case. Neither Mrs Creggan nor Mrs Fairweather could possibly hear her however loudly she screamed. There was no one to help.

No one but herself. 'Get on with it, you fool!' said a voice in her head. She realised that the crushing grip was inexpert, that her attacker had no idea what to do with her next. Suddenly police combat training took over. She slipped out of the man's hold, pushed him away, and with a powerful kick had him floored and winded, a deflated heap on the ground, drawing harsh breaths, while she stood ready to attack him again.

He looked up at her with pale, defeated eyes.

'Well?' she asked him. 'What's the game? And why me?'

Croaking words came out. 'I were only lookin' . . . at first. I saw you once, close. After that I couldn't keep away.'

16

He struggled to one elbow, but she threatened him, and he subsided.

'I'm not a Black Belt,' she told him, 'but I could do you a lot of harm. So, what couldn't you keep away from?'

'You. Missis . . . Inspector. I've never seen owt like you. You look like you could . . . rule the world.'

'Thank you very much. I don't think that's any excuse for breaking into my house.'

He blinked. 'I wanted . . . just to touch you. Yon big chap – I've watched him – he doesn't need you like I do. Look, I've got pictures I've cut out o' t'papers.' Half-sitting, he fumbled in a pocket and produced a scruffy file of folded cuttings. Jean was torn between a desire to laugh and a keen pity. She gave way to neither.

'All right. Get up. Sit on that chair. If you make one move you'll be sorry.' She called Hartley on her personal radio, that always lay on the hall table when she was at home, watching him all the time, but he sat quite still, deflated, his eyes following her like a dog's.

She said, 'A police car will be here in five minutes.'

'What . . . what's going to 'appen to me?'

'How should I know? Depends if you've got a record for this sort of thing.'

He shook his head slowly.

'Then you'd better watch it in future. You do realise you could be up on a serious charge?'

He seemed not to understand, and she realised that he literally couldn't take his eyes off her.

There was nothing that could be said between them. In less time than seemed possible she heard the Ford Escort draw up, and opened the door to admit Bentley and Melchett. Their eyes widened at the sight of her negligée.

'Good,' she said. 'There he is. Take him in, and I'll be down as soon as I'm dressed.'

'Right, Ma'am. Come on, you.' Melchett took the man by the arm and propelled him out, unresisting. At the door he turned.

'I were only lookin', missis,' he said. She watched as they escorted him, none too gently, down the path and into the

17

waiting car. Time was when they'd have had a laugh about their Inspector being a sex-object, vulnerable to the attacks of rapists. Now their attitude was very different. Jean had from the beginning set herself against gestures of chivalry, the opening of car-doors for her, a hand extended to help her up steps. But she had no power over the instinct that lies deep in man to protect woman, Inspector or not. The lurker was not going to be popular at the Nick.

Arnold Brown, aged fifty-two, unemployed, unmarried, a history of job-shirking, two convictions for shop-lifting. He had done nothing in his life, he was nobody. Yet he had the capacity to harm, and the magistrates bound him over with severe warnings about what his fate would be if he were again seen loitering or reported to be pestering women.

'Doesn't help the poor bugger much,' Tom said. 'I wonder if counselling might help . . .'

'You can't help a man like that,' said Jean, 'you ought to know that by now, love. Catch them young, or take them in when they're old and past it, but in between there's nothing. Nothing, only keeping them out of trouble.'

Tom said nothing. He had come to much the same conclusion himself, but still kept the flame burning for the no-hopers, the drop-outs, that came his way in the course of his social work. He had stopped arguing with Jean about such things; it only caused flare-ups between them.

Within a week of the Alma Street affair the rapist was caught. Neighbours were only too glad to report persistent hangings-about by a young man out of a job, with nothing better to do than stare through windows at undressed women; and Shirley Coates hadn't been too particular about drawing her curtains – asking for it, you might say. Which was confirmed by the young man who lived by doing casual work on building sites. 'Thought she wanted it, showin' herself off like that – can't blame me, can you, for gettin' it wrong?' But they did, and he went down for five years.

Jean came away from Court thoughtful. Did you have to suffer a burglary before you could enter into the feelings of the robbed? She had experienced that, in the case of Marilyn Royle and her boyfriend – the feeling of contamination left behind when one's personal possessions have been pawed over, one's innocent secrets uncovered. Now she knew what the ravished felt like, those whose bodies had been at the mercy of another person's will: she had known it at the moment when Arnold Brown's obsessive desire had pinioned her in her own house, and for a flicker of time she had not been a policewoman, only a woman, and frightened.

All a nonsense, of course, when the attacker had been inadequate, pathetic Arnold Brown. And yet the sickened, threatened feeling was with her still, and she was somehow changed; and for a long time she would avoid looking at the spot by the car-park where he had stood, only looking . . .

2 Ask a Policeman

Old Elsie Barlow froze in her tracks at the knock on the door; not a timid rap but a sharp, authoritarian rat-tat with the knocker. It was a sound seldom heard in the place that was Elsie's home, one of a row of ancient almshouses founded by a dead-and-gone alderman of Hartley for the benefit of respectable single women of the parish. Elsie was highly respectable, having been an assistant in an equally dead-and-gone draper's shop in the days when change travelled from counter to cash-desk in a little brass barrel. She was also single, and had been for the whole of her seventy-four years.

Single and solitary: that was how she liked it. Never one for gossip, her commerce with her neighbours was limited to a curt greeting as she holy-stoned the front step of her little fortress. Once a week the milkman rang for his money. Once a week she went for groceries to the shop round the corner, watching the adding up of the bill with a beady eye, for she'd put nothing past these cheeky young girls in the way of fiddling. Once a week she walked in the other direction, to the post office where she collected her pension, then on to the library to change her book. Otherwise she bothered nobody, and they knew better than to bother her. Her small black-and-white television screen was her best friend. As far as she was thankful for anything she was thankful for a good pair of eyes.

So the sudden knock startled her. She went over in her mind the possibilities. Old Mrs Leggatt next door but two might have had another attack. Well, Elsie didn't consider herself strong enough to drag heavy people off the floor; someone else could be found to do that. Or the knocker might be another of these daft folk that tried to make you read some religious pamphlet and prated on at you about the end of the world. Or . . .

The knock was repeated. This time she went to the small high window and edged the lace curtain aside just enough to see who was there. The solid, foursquare bulk of a policeman loomed before her door, at once reassuring and alarming. But, she told herself, he couldn't be bringing news of a disaster, for she had no relations or friends to whom a disaster could have happened, beyond a cousin in Hartlepool that she'd never liked anyway. So it couldn't be like what happened on the telly, when they took their cap off and said, 'Please sit down, ma'am, I'm afraid I've got bad news . . .'

She opened the door.

The policeman was thirtyish, at a guess, tall and broad, with a cheerful, open face. He smiled, and Elsie managed a smile back, unusual for her.

''Morning, Miss Barlow. Can I come in for a minute?'

'Well. Yes, all right.'

He looked round the small room that served her for living and sleeping in. 'My! You've got a cosy little place. I wouldn't mind one like it myself.'

'You won't be getting one,' Elsie replied tartly. 'These are for retired ladies only. And how did you know my name?'

'It's our business to know names, Miss Barlow. I could tell you the name of everybody in this row if you asked me. We like to keep an eye on you all, you know, make sure you're all right.'

Elsie thought of snapping back that the police needn't bother, about her at any rate, because she didn't like eyes on her, theirs or anybody else's. But there was something so frank and friendly in his manner that she only said, 'Well, what do you want?'

'It's this. I don't want to frighten you, but a man's been seen hanging about that alley back of the almshouses – somebody saw him trying to get over the wall. We've kept a check on it but the foot patrol men can't be in two places at once, and there's times when he could be unobserved. Now, once over that wall a determined character wouldn't have much difficulty in breaking down one of these back doors.'

Elsie was not frightened, but she was unpleasantly aware that he might be right. Each almshouse ended in a lean-to kitchenette with a door into a yard containing a privy, one to each house, and a dustbin which had to be carried through to the front on collection days. A fairly low wall separated the yards from a narrow alley know as Lantern Lane, possibly first so called by some wag because there were no lights in it. It was popular with courting couples (Elsie had been known to reproach them sternly from her yard, and had received some rude answers back) and with winos, who found it a nice private place to linger in with a bottle.

'You do keep your back door bolted, Miss Barlow?'

Elsie hesitated. It was inconvenient to have to draw the bolts every time she visited the privy or put rubbish in the dustbin. 'Well, I always keep the latch down.'

He shook his head. 'Not enough. These customers know all about opening doors with credit cards, that sort of thing. If the bolt's drawn you'd have that much more time to go out at the front and raise the alarm. Do you mind if I have a look at the door?'

'If you want to. Through there.'

She watched him in the kitchenette, tut-tutting over the fragile door and door-furniture installed perhaps ninety years before, perhaps longer. He came back.

'He'd not have much trouble with that. One good push at it and the hinges'd give. You want a better lock, for a start. Now, I'd like to go outside and have a good look at that wall. There might be some way of making it more secure.'

'Spikes or broken glass?' Elsie suggested. He smiled.

'A bit old-fashioned these days – I think we could come up with something more sophisticated.'

He was out in the yard some time. Elsie stayed indoors because of the cold. Reluctant as she was to entertain company, she admitted to herself that there was a certain comfort in knowing that you were looked after, and by people so pleasant and competent. Unaccustomed stirrings of hospitality prompted her, when he came back, to ask him if he would like a cup of tea. He beamed.

'You know, I was just wondering if I dared ask. It's like

Christmas out there. Very kind of you, if it's not too much trouble.'

'No trouble.' She went into the kitchen. Visitors were so rare that she had to look round for suitable crockery, finally deciding on two cups and saucers that had belonged to her mother. They stood on a high shelf and had gathered dust. She washed and dried them carefully, then put the heavy old tin kettle on the gas-cooker. Anybody else would have bought a smaller, modern kettle, but Elsie saw no reason for spending money unnecessarily. At the bottom of the biscuit barrel a few rather elderly digestives remained. She decided they were good enough to present, and washed a plate that matched the china. Altogether, quite a ceremonial. When she went back into the sitting-room with the laden tray she felt like a society hostess. The policeman had taken off his chequer-banded cap; he looked quite boyish without it. He seemed to enjoy the cheap brand of tea, asking for a second cup, and appeared not to notice that the biscuits were stale. Elsie asked him about his work; he told her an exciting story of a roof-top chase and the final capture of two villains, another of a householder found murdered not many streets away, all because his doors weren't properly secured. The clock struck twelve noon. He checked it with his watch.

'Time I was off. I've got to report back. Thanks ever so much for the tea, Miss Barlow. I'll be back when we've worked out what to do about that wall.'

At the door she asked, 'Are you going to all the houses along here?'

'That's right. I'll have to come back, though. I didn't reckon on spending so much time with you.'

It wouldn't have occured to Elsie to return 'You're welcome,' in the way of Americans, but she murmured something reasonably gracious. When he had gone she bolted both front and back doors, and stood looking through the window over the sink at the wall that threatened her peace. You never knew where trouble was coming from. What would they do to make it safe? Something with electric current?

Suddenly she realised that her routine had been thrown

out by the visitor. It was half-day closing, she just had to get to the shop and make her usual deliberate purchases. Hastily she tidied away the tray and its contents, put on her coat and hat and switched off her single-bar fire, before checking her purse.

It was empty. There had been almost a poundsworth of loose change in it, all gone. Frantically she looked inside the compartment that held bank-notes; it, too, was empty. All her week's pension money had been in it, collected two days before and untouched. Cold with horror, she scrabbled through the rest of the bag, the part where she kept her handkerchief and reading-glasses, the special bit for keys and oddments, in case the money had by some mysterious process got into them. It hadn't.

Could she have forgetfully put it into the old silver box that had belonged to her father, on the table where her handbag was always kept? If she had, it had doubly vanished, for the box too was gone – her treasure, one of the few good things she owned, always kept polished and bright.

It was years since Elsie had cried, but now she did, tears of shock and distress coursing down her wrinkled cheeks. Robbed of every penny she had in the place – nothing left for her shopping, nothing to put into her post office savings account on Friday (for she had never trusted banks). And by that . . . as she thought of the policeman her tears dried up, and fury took over.

Sergeant Beck had taken advantage of comparative mid-day quiet to have a telephone chat with a pal in CID. Beck was less keen on the horses than George Parrish, but he liked the occasional flutter and his pal was often good for a tip.

'The two-thirty,' he said. 'What d'you reckon? Sixteen running. I fancy Tartan Lad myself, but . . .' His back was to the door, so he didn't see it open. He spun round as the telephone receiver was snatched from his hand and replaced in its cradle with a bang. He was looking down, bewildered, into the contorted face of a small elderly woman, and she was glaring up at him.

'You can stop that!' she shouted. '*I* heard you – betting on horses, just the sort of thing your sort do. Police! don't talk to me about police!'

'I wasn't going to,' Beck interrupted mildly. 'Do you mind telling me what your business is?'

'You know very well. Where is it – come on now, where is it?'

Beck shook his head like a bull troubled by the picador's darts. 'I don't follow you, madam. Where's what?' He summed her up as a loose nut, probably dangerous with it if she got hold of anything lethal. Unobtrusively he moved a heavy paper-weight and a metal anglepoise lamp out of her way. She brandished her fists at him.

'My money. You've got my money and my box, and I want them back!' Sudden doubt came into her face. 'But – you're not him, are you?'

Patiently Beck drew forward his day-book. 'No, I shouldn't think I am. Now can we get it all clear? Name please.'

But she was staring at Melchett, who had appeared from the parade room. 'There he is! He's done something to his face, but he can't fool me. What have you done with my money, you dirty thief?'

They were all talking at once, Melchett protesting, Beck trying to stop Elsie's accusations. Jean came out of her office.

'What on earth's going on here? Be quiet, all of you. Now, Sergeant Beck.'

'This lady seems to be under a bit of a misapprehension, Ma'am. Says she's had some money stolen and seems to think it was one of us.'

Jean said, without blinking, 'Then we'd better get the facts down, hadn't we.'

'That's what I've been trying to do, Ma'am. If I *could* have your name, Miss . . .'

'My name's Miss Elsie Barlow and I live at Ryall's Alms-houses, not that I need to tell *you* that since it's your business to know – that's what *he* said.' She pointed to the baffled Melchett, and turned on Jean. 'And I don't need you to interfere, miss, whoever you may be, all dressed up like *he* was though I don't suppose you're any better than a typist, with your face painted like a street-woman . . .'

Beck and Melchett carefully avoided catching Jean's eye,

but she said without a flicker of reaction, 'I think this needs sorting out, Miss Barlow – and in fact I'm Inspector Darblay, in charge of this section. You say you've been robbed, by Detective Sergeant Melchett here?'

'Well, I think it was him – only he had his jacket on, and one of those caps with checks round.'

'Ma'am,' said Melchett, now pink with annoyance, 'I only came on duty half an hour ago and I've been here ever since. Sergeant Beck will confirm that.'

'I'm sure we can take that as read, Sergeant. Perhaps you and Miss Barlow had better come into my office.'

Elsie sat on the edge of the interviewee's chair, staring resentfully round Jean's office. She'd come to the police station to accuse her thief, get her property back and say a few words about the whole corrupt lot, not to be questioned as if she was the guilty one by a jumped-up young woman in a collar and tie. She could see that she wouldn't get any justice here; they were all hand in glove with one another, thieves of a feather flocking together.

'So,' said Jean, writing, 'you opened the door because you saw a policeman outside.'

'Well, I thought it was safe to let a policeman in, little thinking . . .'

'We'll come to that. What was this man wearing?'

'A uniform – I told you.'

'Did he give you his name?'

'Name? I don't think so.'

'Did you notice his number, and the letter of this division? in metal, on his shoulder?'

'No.'

'Did he carry a personal radio?'

'A what? You mean one of those walkie-talkie things?'

'Yes.'

Doubt flickered across Elsie's face. 'Well . . . I didn't notice.'

'He showed you his warrant card, of course.'

'No, he didn't show me any sort of card.'

Jean sighed. 'You should always ask to see a warrant card if one isn't produced instantly, as it should be, by a policeman seeking entry.' She exchanged a glance with Melchett. 'And what happened then?'

Sulkily, feeling herself losing ground, Elsie described the conversation and the visitor's inspection of her yard. 'When he came back I offered to make him a cup of tea. That was when it happened, when I went to the kitchen.'

'Leaving him alone?'

'That's right. My handbag was on the table, next to the silver presentation box, and when I came to look in it after that devil had gone there was no money in it at all, not a penny left, and father's box gone too.' Suddenly her old face crumpled. Jean watched her fumbling blindly in the rifled bag for a handkerchief, then handed over her own, immaculately laundered and pressed. Melchett watched, knowing almost to a word what she would say next, so closely had the men under her command come to know her.

She leaned forward. 'Miss Barlow. It's quite clear to me that you've been taken in by someone impersonating a police officer.'

'But he had the uniform on . . .' Elsie snuffled.

'Uniforms can be hired – more's the pity. You'll have to accept that neither Sergeant Melchett nor any other officer of this section had any connection with the robbery. It's a well-known trick, playing at policemen, though usually for bigger game than private theft. Security patrols, bank breaks, that sort of thing. I can't tell you what chance we have of finding the man, but it may comfort you to know that if we do we can have him on a serious count.'

Melchett recited mentally a still-existing act of 1839 ' . . .who shall put on the dress, or take the name, designation, or character of any person appointed as a constable, for the purpose of thereby obtaining admission into any house or other place . . .' There was a later act, imposing a fine of £10 merely for wearing a police uniform, except on the stage.

'Shall you get it back for me?' Elsie quavered. She had abandoned her fight. The police were quite unlike the chatty man with his made-up story, and the young woman seemed to have a good head on her.

'That I can't say. It's not very likely, I'm afraid. But we'll try. Are you feeling all right, Miss Barlow?'

She was feeling far from all right, shaky in the legs, weakly ashamed of crying in public, very much alone. Melchett didn't need Jean's expressive glance and nod to take her away to the Interview Room and administer a cup of tea. Beck drifted in and chatted. Soon she began to feel better, cared for and protected, the way she'd so mistakenly felt in the morning. Somebody came in and asked her to describe the thief, his face, the way his hair grew, his eyes; and, a bit later, came back with a drawing that was really very like him.

'You're very clever,' Elsie said, and, when Melchett drove her home, 'Thank you very much.' He watched her let herself in and bolt the door behind her.

They traced the uniform to a costumier in Manchester. The old-established firm kept careful records of where its costumes went; there had been one single uniform with no stage or television use recorded against it, only the name A. Conran, and an address which turned out to be false. The sharp-eyed young man in charge of the men's department recognised the photofit portrait instantly. 'That's him, to a T. I can give you his measurements if you like.'

The measurements weren't needed, because the face was familiar. Impersonation was Alec Conran's strong suit (he had even been brash enough to give his own name). Gas and electricity meter-readers, deputy rent-collectors, were his favourite characters, but he also had a line in being taken suddenly ill in shops and collaring the till while whoever was behind the counter went for help. He had worked successfully at a 'Blind Persons Crossing' spot, painlessly removing the handbags and wallets of such blind persons as were foolish enough to trust him. Armed with a neatly printed card and an impeccable notebook, giving details of subscribers and amounts, he had begged from door to door for a wholly non-existent charity.

They caught him at a house on the edge of the Yorkshire Moors, a stately pile maintained by the income of a proprietor of a chain of restaurants. It so happened that when the smiling character wearing a dog-collar appeared at the porticoed front door it was opened by the proprietor's lady. Gimlet-eyed, herself a graduate from big business, she invited him into the hall and disappeared, presumably to fetch her handbag. He was gratified when a maid appeared with coffee for him; less so when a constable, wearing authentic uniform, rang the front door bell.

A search of Conran's rooms revealed the still unsold silver box, tarnished now, inscribed 'To R. S. Barlow, Esq., on the occasion of his retirement.' Jean took it round personally to the almshouses, wearing plain clothes. There was no answer to her repeated knocks. Only after knocking for a full five minutes she saw an eye peer round the lace curtain. Smiling she held up the box.

'Where's the money?' Elsie asked.

'Sorry we couldn't trace that. But he got five years, if that's any comfort to you.'

'I don't know that it is,' said Elsie, and shut the door in Jean's face. They'd buttered her up at the police station all right, but the butter had worn off now, she'd never trust them again.

Even when they came within minutes of a neighbour raising the alarm, after a youth had climbed over the yard-wall and kicked in the frail old door, to rob Elsie of every trifle of value she possessed; just as the fake policeman had said would happen.

3 I'll Not Forget Old Ireland

Joseph Beck leant on the deck-rail, looking back towards the Heysham shore, the winking lighthouse and the dark tumbled boulders where once he had played as a child, paddling in the clear rock-pools, collecting shells and stones, avoiding with his bare feet the jelly-fish that sometimes lay, transparent, in wait for unwary children.

Forty years ago. He remembered the coastal defences, barbed wire and concrete, after the war had begun. And further back, how Morecambe had seemed like the fun-centre of the world in contrast with Preston, where he lived: the famous Italian ice-cream shop on the prom, the melting saltiness of oysters, the thrills of the permanent fairground, the roundabout whose steeds were fierce-looking painted horses with flaring nostrils, the switchback and the figure eight with its cars full of shrieking girls. Walking with his father across the shining silver sand of the Fishing Grounds when the tide was out. Tea with his mother at some little garden place in Heysham; scrambling around the Saxon stone coffins, and the little church that was supposed to have been founded by Saint Patrick, taking time off from converting Ireland.

Ireland. He had to go all the way to Ireland to see Carol. Once he had imagined taking her to Morecambe as he had been taken, introducing her to the pleasures which must still be there for a child. But that hadn't suited Marcia at all. They'd had to go down south for their holidays, to places like Torquay and Eastbourne that she thought better class, and that Beck found snobbish and alien. And then, when Carol was only six, the break had come.

It had been the old, old story. A wife sick of police hours, himself furious at finding she'd been out on dates with other men, leaving Carol to any baby-sitter she could get – almost nightly quarrels that the child couldn't help but hear, and got upset about. His own temper hadn't helped; he'd learned to control it behind a mask of impassivity now, when it was too late.

For Marcia had been awarded custody of Carol. They'd said a policeman couldn't possibly look after a child properly. It hadn't influenced them that his daughter was all he cared about in the world, now that Marcia and he were like strangers, or that she adored her father and had cried for three days when he left the house to live in digs. And then Marcia had taken her away, to live with her parents in County Antrim, and he saw her about four times a year.

It would have been quicker and easier to have flown from Ringway, but Beck had a fear of flying that he mentioned to nobody, despising himself for a weakness he couldn't help. He preferred the train and the boat, enjoying the enforced leisure away from Hartley, the scenery rushing by, drinks in the saloon; and time to think about seeing Carol again. She'd have changed, just that little bit. The Mandy doll he had given her last time would be laid aside, because it was all ballet with her now. In his suitcase were a pair of practice tights and a charming little tutu which he'd bought in Manchester, assured by the saleswoman that it couldn't help but fit a slim little girl of Carol's age. And there was a book about Fonteyn, second-hand but recommended to him as a must for ballet-mad people.

Half-past eleven. He looked round at the dark sea, the ship's wake rippling in moonlight, the dim shape of the Isle of Man ahead. Time to get some sleep. The last thing he visualised in his narrow bunk was Carol being a little older, himself living in a decent house with a decent woman cooking and caretaking, Carol coming to stay with him, being there when he got home after a stretch on duty . . .

At last he was there, in the grey 1910-ish house in a village that looked across to the Antrim Mountains. The village was grey, too, plain-faced in a peculiarly Irish way, as though all the beauty had gone into the scenery and none into the

31

architecture. They were having tea, he and Marcia and Carol, dropped scones and honey, home-made sponge cakes and biscuits. Beck's eyes were on his daughter, curled on a bean-bag by the fender, her long legs tucked under her. She was taller and thinner: he worried about the fitting of the tights. Little hollows sculpted her cheeks, and he wondered, not for the first time, where the delicate moulding of her face had come from. Not from him, four-square-featured and heavily fleshed, or from Marcia, round-cheeked as a doll.

Carol had greeted him with a close embrace, arms tight round his neck. Then, as he thought of it, she went quiet. Marcia was doing all the talking, chattering away.

'I must say, we're lucky to be this far outside Belfast. More trouble yesterday, did you see?'

He had seen. The news from Northern Ireland was the first thing he turned to in the paper. 'Nothing near here, though?'

'Not a sign. There aren't any borders, of course, or anyone they might be gunning for.' She laughed. 'I didn't mean quite that, but I suppose it fits . . . You don't need to worry, really, Joe.'

He couldn't help but worry, knowing of the bus that took Carol and other kids to and from the school about five miles away. Might it one morning or afternoon be ambushed, explosives hidden underneath it, for no better reason than one of the kids had an English policeman for a father? He switched the thought off.

'How's the ballet going?'

Carol said, 'All right.' Marcia interrupted, chattering again. He knew that she was nervous about something.

'Well, they seem very pleased with her, but there's just this worry that she might get too tall, after the way she's grown this year. I shouldn't be surprised, really – I mean, look at you, and I'm not small. Still, Miss Shaw did say that people like Moira Fraser had done all right –'

'For Lilac Fairies and things,' Carol said flatly. 'She couldn't dance the *real* roles, once she got so tall.'

Beck, who had never seen a ballet in his life, said 'I suppose not.' He was studying his daughter's withdrawn face, turned to the fire, his ex-wife's obviously new and expensive-looking dress, her dark hair recently set in a style that made her look much younger than her thirty-seven years. Twelve years less than his own age; what a fool he'd been not to realise that was a mistake. Good police wives didn't grow on trees.

'How's Hartley?' she was asking. 'Funny old Hartley.'

'Much the same as usual.'

'Still got your female Inspector?'

'That's right.'

'Oh, you've not frightened her away yet?'

'We get on.' He saw the flash of impatience in her face at his laconic way of talking. She was trying to make light conversation, leading up to something, whatever it might be. He sensed tension in the room from both of them, and was glad he didn't have to do verbal battle with her parents, as well. After the marriage break-up they had made the house into two flats, Marcia and Carol having the top one. It hadn't been done for his benefit; he had not been Marcia's parents' choice for their girl, and he knew they would be glad if he stopped visiting his daughter. Marcia herself would be glad of it too, she usually made that very plain – but for some reason she'd set herself out to be agreeable this time. Why?

Carol suddenly said, 'I've got to go and do my homework now.'

Beck was disappointed. 'Can't you put it off for a bit?'

'Don't say that to her,' Marcia broke in, 'it's hard enough to get her to do it usually. Off you go, dear – shut the door so we won't disturb you, talking.'

Beck thought wistfully of his suitcase in the hall, and the parcel in it which he had been planning to give Carol after the tea ritual was over, and watch her delight as she opened it. Now it would have to wait until much later, when the excitement of his arrival had worn off. Not that it had been very exciting. For the first time that special light had not been in her eyes.

When she had left the room he said, 'Let's talk, then.'

'Talk?'

'That's what you told her we were going to do.' He could

hear his own voice in the Interview Room, waiting for a reluctant interviewee to give out with information. Marcia was going through her little putting-it-off tricks, fiddling with an ear-ring, plaiting the stuff of her skirt into folds. At last she said, 'Joe, I'm going to get married again.'

'You – what?'

She was instantly defensive. 'Well, you didn't think I was going to hang about like this all the rest of my life, did you? Not exactly past it yet, am I? Or perhaps you think I am?'

Beck stared at her, trying to collect himself. He hadn't thought of such a possibility: though why not? Marcia was not a Catholic, and even if she had been, and wanted something very badly, she would have got round it somehow, if it meant arguing with the Pope. But he was shaken, trying hard to take in the implications. He didn't want her back, they could never live together again, and yet . . .

He said, 'I don't think you're past it, no. It's just that – you didn't say anything last time you wrote.'

Marcia shrugged. 'It's not easy, putting things on paper.'

'So. What about it, then?'

'Well, he's called Denis O'Gorman. He works in insurance.'

'Nice regular hours?'

'No need to be sarcastic. He works at their head office in Cushendall. We've seen a fabulous flat there, right on the sea, looking out over the bay, really smashing.'

'Good,' said Beck heavily. Evidently it was all happening, everything sewn up, whether he liked it or not. He was beginning not to like it.

'What about Carol's school?'

'Oh, she'll have to move, of course. There's quite a good one there.'

'Been to see it, have you?'

'Well, no, not yet. It's a bit early to bother about that.'

'I'd have thought it was the first thing to bother about. She's getting on well where she is now, isn't she?'

'Yes, but at that age –'

'Just the age not to move her, wouldn't you say, with the exam coming up next year?'

34

'You're just making difficulties!' Marcia snapped. 'Carol, Carol, always Carol, not a thought for me and my happiness, and God knows I didn't have much with you. I'm marrying Denis whether you like it or not, and Carol will just have to fit in.'

Beck felt one of his old surges of temper coming on. He got up, noisily putting down the cup and saucer and plate he had been unconsciously balancing. A bull in a china shop, that was how Marcia made him feel.

'I'm going to unpack,' he said. At the door he turned back. 'There's one thing you forgot to say.'

'Well, what?'

'Be glad for me.'

In the spare bedroom he unpacked his suitcase. The parcel was there, wrapped in pretty paper from the shop. Last time he had looked at it he had been full of excited anticipation, all vanished now.

Carol was in her bedroom, sitting at a table spread with books. She looked up as he entered, her smile only touching her mouth, not her eyes.

'Busy?' he asked.

'Well, I'm a bit stuck.'

'Give it a miss and see what I've brought you.'

He watched her take off the wrappings. When she came to the contents surprised pleasure flickered across her face, a spark quickly dying.

'Thanks, Dad. Lovely.'

'Aren't you going to try it on, the skirt thing? They said it would fit, but if it doesn't I can take it back.'

Carol tied the tutu round her waist, over her jeans and tee-shirt.

'It's just right. Great. Thanks again, Dad.' She gave him a perfunctory hug, but he held her.

'What's the matter, love? I thought you'd be over the moon about it. Not gone off ballet, have you?'

'Oh no! I want to be a dancer, more than anything. Only – I've got to go to a new school next term. It's miles and miles away, so I can't keep on with Miss Shaw. So it's not much use really.'

'Don't they have ballet classes, at this new school?'

'I don't know. And it wouldn't be the same as Miss Shaw, anyway.'

Beck was silent. He felt that something beautiful was being destroyed in front of his eyes.

'This chap,' he said, 'whatshisname, mum's told me about. What d'you think of him?'

Carol looked away. 'He's all right.'

'What sort of all right?'

Her lip quivered, and she burst into tears, throwing herself into his arms, her face pressed into his shoulder as it had always been when she came to him for consolation. 'It won't be like it was,' she sobbed.

'Here, here, here.' He patted her back. 'What's all this? What won't be like it was?'

'You. You're my dad, he's not. You won't come any more . . .' She clung to him, weeping, unable to express her misery. He held her, crushing the neglected tutu. It was true. Another man would have the right to call himself Carol's father, and his visits to her would have to be arranged in some awkward fashion, meeting in a café, staying at an hotel with her for the weekend, no longer a member, even temporarily, of the household. As he put her arm from him gently she looked up with swimming eyes.

'Can't you do anything, Dad?'

'No. There's nowt I can do, love. We'll have to make the best of it, won't we.'

Marcia had switched the television on when he went back into the sitting-room. Silently they watched the News – more bomb outrages, a climbing accident in the mountains, the racing results. Beck neither knew nor cared what he was watching. When it was over Marcia said, 'He's coming round this evening – Denis. I thought it would be nice for you to meet him. Oh, I can see you don't want to and you're right sour about the whole thing, but there it is, Joe, you'll have to like it or lump it.'

'I'm going for a walk.'

He tramped doggedly round the ugly village, whose only charm was the view it had of mountains more blue and misty than the heights that looked down to Hartley. He couldn't remember having been so unhappy since the day he had seen Carol off for Ireland, the first time. And it was true what he had said to her – there was nothing he could do.

Marcia had changed into an evening pants-suit a little too young and tight for her, and her perfume was powerful. On the stroke of seven a car pulled into the circular drive and was heard to stop.

'There he is!' she cried. Like a girl she ran to the window and waved.

Denis O'Gorman was good-looking in a black-haired, red-cheeked fashion (tuppence coloured, thought Beck grimly) and obviously younger than Marcia. He had a pronounced Belfast accent and a toothy grin. Their meeting, potentially embarrassing, seemed not to disconcert him at all; it was Beck who dropped the proffered hand quickly, murmuring in reply to the 'Pleased to meet you.' O'Gorman kissed Marcia, a long, show-off kiss; Beck saw her glance obliquely at him over O'Gorman's shoulder, a glance with a glint of triumph in it. A twinge of the old jealousy stirred in him.

'Now, shall we have a drink?' she suggested brightly. O'Gorman slapped her bottom, his usual mode of caress.

'That's my girl. She doesn't hang about, does she , . .' Beck knew that he was waiting to be prompted to call him Joe. He merely stared back, his eyes reduced to slits with a beady glint in them. Colleagues and villains had frequently seen him look like that.

The drink was sherry, something Beck loathed, and he suspected that O'Gorman wasn't fond of it either, from the way he toyed with his glass. Long ago Marcia and he had quarrelled about his habit of having beer with his meals and whenever drink was called for. It wasn't a nice thing to drink, she said, it smelt awful – if he wanted it he must go and swill it with his mates in pubs. Which was what he had done.

Between sips of the cloying sherry O'Gorman and Marcia chatted; Beck could tell they were trying to out-smart each other in repartee. O'Gorman turned to him. 'Follow the dogs at all, do you?'

'No I don't.'

Joe prefers horses,' Marcia said. Carol sidled into the room, unnoticed by anyone but her father, and stood uncertainly, waiting.

'Give me the whelps every time,' O'Gorman said. 'They're a whole lot of fun, the way a horse isn't. My pal Mike – you know Mike Donovan, Marce – he's got a dog, Ballyclare Boy — the fastest pup on legs and next thing to a man-eating tiger. You know, last time I was over at his place Mike let Boy off the lead, for a bit of a run – saw a cat, had it before it could turn round – snapped its head off like a fox with a chicken.'

Marcia laughed. Beck saw Carol's face and went to her side.

'Don't take any notice,' he said softly. 'All tall stories. Like fishermen tell.' But she looked white and sick; and O'Gorman had heard him, as had Marcia.

'Carol, you're being silly again. Don't be such a baby!'

O'Gorman suddenly grabbed at Carol's hand and pulled her towards him. 'You'll have to learn to be a sport, girl, won't you. Got to be tough in this world, you know. Want to come and see the dogs run on Saturday?'

'No,' Carol said. 'I hate dogs. I'll go to Maeve's, like I always do.'

'Suit yourself.' O'Gorman administered a sharp unkind pinch to her cheek before pushing her away. Beck watched the flush come up on the pale skin, and her wince of pain, and knew the rising of such a rage as he hadn't felt since the time when he and Marcia had been married.

'Mr O'Gorman,' he said, slowly and deliberately, 'I reckon you and I could do with a pint. There's a bar down the village. Come on.'

'But we're going to have supper!' Marcia exclaimed. 'You don't want to go out now . . .'

'I do,' Beck said.

'Denis?'

O'Gorman shrugged. 'Doesn't matter to me.' His look at her said that she'd wanted this meeting and he'd go along with whatever this ex of hers was about. Outside, Beck said nothing and O'Gorman didn't know what he could add to that. They walked silently along the empty street to where a sign said BAR. It was on the lines of an Eire drinking-house, the front a shop still serving groceries and dry goods, the back room with a fire in the grate and an old man serving drinks to a few customers, who turned enquiring glances on Beck, the stranger.

O'Gorman pulled out some coins. 'They've got some good Irish here.'

'No, thanks. I'm paying.'

'Oh, well. Jameson's.'

Beck asked for an Irish whiskey and a half of Guinness. O'Gorman glanced at an empty table, but Beck remained standing.

'Well, let's have it,' O'Gorman said. 'This is just a friendly jar, is it?'

'No, it isn't. I want a word with you. What's your attitude to my daughter?'

'Carol?'

'Don't know of another.'

'Bloody funny question, then. She's my future wife's kid, isn't she?'

'That's not the point. Do you like her? Are you fond of her?'

'Bloody funnier question. Kids are kids, aren't they. One day they'll grow up.'

'Into human beings? That's what you meant, isn't it. I heard the way you spoke to her, and I saw the pinch you gave her. She didn't like that, or the cat-and-dog story. Neither did I.'

O'Gorman stopped smiling. Beck noted that his mouth, red like his cheeks, was full-shaped and yet had a cruel look to it. 'This is about Marce, isn't it,' he said. 'Jealous husband, younger rival.' He looked Beck up and down. 'Can't say I blame her, from where I'm standing.'

Beck was not interested in insults. 'It's nothing to do with Marcia. She can pick who she likes. It's my daughter's future I'm concerned with. Is she going to be treated like I treat her, or pushed on one side? This place where you're going – have you thought what's in it for her, how she'll like being rooted up from her school and sent to a different one?'

'What the hell's that got to do with me? It's Marce's worry.'

'Not yours at all – you've got no responsibility?'

'No!' O'Gorman almost shouted, and heads turned. 'I'm marrying a woman, not a daddy's girl with a face like a sick cat. If you want her, you take her!'

The smoky room, and the man a foot or so away from him, and the gawping mouths, blurred together in a red haze. In that moment he was neither a sergeant nor even a policeman or a rational person, but an angry beast defending its young, as he smashed his fist into O'Gorman's jaw. Unprepared, O'Gorman fell backwards, knocking over a chair and scattering glasses from a table. Beck was not aware, until the moment had passed, of what he had done. He stood, dazed, amid the scene of confusion, raised voices, a knot of men crowding round the prostrate O'Gorman, liquor flowing over the red floor-covering, a different red showing at the corner of O'Gorman's mouth, running down his chin.

Voices were shouting at him, arms pulling at him, rocking him almost off his balance. Someone was saying, 'Police! send for the police.' But that meant himself; the policeman, guardian of law and order, who had just committed a serious assault on a member of the public. None of this could really be happening to him.

When the young constable from the station Beck had noticed at the end of the street arrived O'Gorman had not moved. The barman was trying to force brandy between his lips.

'You don't want to do that,' Beck said. 'Keep his head flat and cover him up with something. Here –' He took off his own overcoat.

'Look who's talking!' said the barman. 'What did you want to half-kill the feller for?'

Beck shook his head. A ferret-faced little man who was enjoying every minute of the incident came forward as a spokesman. 'Dropped him like an ox, Jimmy, just for the man raisin' his voice to him . . .'

'Been drinking, had they?' the constable asked.

'I hadn't touched a drop,' Beck said. 'There's mine.' He pointed to his full tankard.

'Drinking somewhere else, then?'

'I'd a few sups of sherry at my . . . at a private house. Not even a full glass.'

'Do you say?' The constable's sandy eyebrows rose unbelievingly. 'All right, I'm arresting you on a charge of assault occasioning actual bodily harm. Come on.' Beck realised, as one in a nightmare sees a nameless horror looming over him, that he was having his collar felt.

They were telephoning for an ambulance for O'Gorman. The constable was claiming two witnesses from those who demanded a hearing. Then the little band set off up the chilly, darkening street towards the Nick.

Constable O'Ferrall was puzzled. The man at his side wasn't behaving in the usual pattern. He had committed a fairly typical drunken assault, but he was not drunk. He should have resisted arrest, protested at being taken in, asked what was going to happen to him. Instead, he was walking along at O'Ferrall's side, apparently lost in his own thoughts, ignoring his escort and the chattering witnesses. Funny sort of customer.

Beck looked round with interest at the village Nick. It was about a quarter of the size of the one at Hartley, a sort of glorified double-fronted cottage with an extension at the back which probably contained cells. The desk sergeant, an ageing man with a mournful moustache, looked up almos⁺ eagerly as O'Ferrall entered with his captive. D. and d. was about the most common offence in those parts; it wasn't exciting but it made a change from sitting around.

Beck gave him a nod (unusual, thought Sergeant Stephens) and followed O'Ferrall into the Interview Room almost before the constable had asked him to do so. If Beck had wished to swing a cat, whatever that curious exercise might involve, he wouldn't have been able to manage it in that tiny, poky, ill-lit place. He took his seat on one side of the table without being asked, causing O'Ferrall to stare. He should have looked round him in surprise, alarm, ignorance, instead of appearing as calm as O'Ferrall himself.

The constable went out and spoke to the sergeant; Beck heard their conversation.

'Don't know what you'll make of this one, Sarge – seems as much at home here as I am.'

'Yeh. Looked the same to me. Punch-up, was it?'

'Seems like it. Not a fight, just one blow, pretty well aimed. And no smell of drink.'

'Well, well. I'm going to enjoy this, Ed.'

The clouds in Beck's mind suddenly cleared, an icy coldness taking their place. He was giving himself away by everything he did, or didn't do. If he went on like this they'd know without doubt that he was a policeman. He had supposed, in the first moments after striking the blow, that it would inevitably come out – that he would have to admit it. But now, in this crummy Nick with these two fairly harmless characters running it, the thought came to him that he might, just, lie or bluff his way out of it. Somehow.

When Sergeant Stephens, glowing with mild enthusiasm, sat down opposite him with paper and pen, he gave his name with not too much readiness.

'Occupation?'

He thought for a second, then said, boot-faced, 'Government officer.'

4 The Leopard's Spots

As though outside his own body, listening, he heard himself testify, in as bumbling a fashion as he could muster, that he had met the man he had attacked through a third party, and that a dispute had quickly arisen between them in which he had lost his temper and lashed out. Yes, he'd had a certain amount of boxing practice. No previous convictions. No police record in England. Over in Antrim to see his divorced wife.

Sergeant Stephens' eyes brightened. 'Your wife any connection with the assault?'

It might provide a believable motive. 'Yes . . .'

The sergeant was writing. ' . . . jealousy.'

Beck looked up from the cool cup of tea they'd brought him. 'If I could see her, soon as possible.' He gave the address.

'Not tonight, son. Tomorrow will do nicely.'

He was lying on one of the narrow hard bunks he knew well, minus his shoes, belt and the contents of his pockets. He prayed they wouldn't go through his wallet and find the warrant card. He lay awake, cold, shocked, seeing on the darkened ceiling visions of his damaged reputation relayed to Hartley, of the waves it would cause: seeing in large illuminated letters the first clause of the Discipline Code.

Discreditable Conduct. That is to say, if he acts in a disorderly manner or any manner prejudicial to discipline or reasonably likely to bring discredit on the reputation of the force or the public service.

And then the charge. Questions in the Discipline Form to be answered by Accused. Procedure at Hearing. Inadmissibility of Personal Explanations at Hearing. Reference to Accused's Personal Record in considering Punishment. He recited them mentally over and over, not knowing at what phrase he fell asleep.

They brought him breakfast, the sort he'd so often seen served to others, only this time the eggs were golden, new-laid, and the toast made from fresh barm-bread. When he was dressed and had shaved with a borrowed razor, he was taken from the cold cell to the Interview Room, such as it was, and told to wait, by another fresh-faced young constable with a thick accent. His reputation had evidently been handed on from the previous night, for he was looked at hard. The new desk sergeant glanced in with a good-morning.

'Comfortable night had you?'

'Yes, thanks.'

The sergeant edged in. 'Seem to have seen you somewhere, haven't I?'

Beck panicked. Could the man by any evil chance have visited Hartley? Had they been at the same police function? The saving memory came to him that it was not his first time in the village, that the sergeant could have seen him strolling in the street, taking Carol to school or meeting her.

'I come here now and then,' he said. It seemed to satisfy.

There were sounds through the shut door, an entry, greetings, murmurs that he couldn't make out however hard he strained his ears. Then the door opened again.

The new arrival was perhaps Beck's own age, neat-figured and spry, grizzle-haired and sharp-eyed, with an un-mistakable air of authority. Beck stood up, afterwards quickly cursing himself for the give-away.

''Morning. Inspector Mullins of Ballyshane.'

'Good morning . . . sir.' It had come out before he could stop himself. In the next fraction of a second he saw it registered in the other man's face, saw his own reaction mirrored there. As the Inspector sat down, so did he, eyes locked until the Inspector smiled and sat back, arms folded.

'Well, now. I hear there was a bit of an affray last night,

and you smote a fellow mightily. Not hip and thigh perhaps, but right on the jaw. You may be pleased to hear that he passed a good night and was discharged this morning.'

Beck nodded. He was glad.

'There seem to have been some unusual features about the assault. Very rapid, I hear, you'd not been in the bar above five minutes. I take it there'd been a previous argument – disagreement – something of that kind?'

'Some bad feeling, yes.' Beck was trying to say as little as possible.

'Known him long?'

'No.'

'How long?'

'Yesterday.'

'Ah.' The Inspector caressed his chin. 'Very sudden, wasn't it?'

Beck said nothing.

'And you're ... Joseph Beck, of Burnley, Lancashire. Now, Constable Beck – or is it Sergeant?'

Beck met his look squarely. 'Sergeant.'

'Thank you. It was bound to come out, you know. I'm glad you told me. What about telling me the rest of it?'

Beck was not in the habit of pouring out confidences. But, trapped between desperation and a sort of relief that he needn't try to act any longer, he began in his own dry well-ordered way to relate the break-up of his marriage, his visits to Carol, the news he had heard the day before. He said nothing of his feelings for his daughter, and was not aware that they spilled out from the factual narrative like seeds from a pomegranate.

'And then I hit him,' he concluded.

Inspector Mullins drew faces on a notepad. 'Without real provocation?'

'Words can be provocation.'

'It wasn't very wise, was it, Sergeant? Might have been wiser in the first place to conduct your argument in private.'

'I didn't want to upset her – my daughter. She's put up with enough.'

45

'I see. And you weren't drunk – you didn't take him to the bar in order to work yourself up with a few jars?'

'I wouldn't do that, sir.'

'No. I expect you'd look on it as something like drinking on duty?'

' A bit like that '

There was a long silence, during which Beck heard the ringing of a telephone, the lowing of cows somewhere at the back of the cells, someone laughing. He hoped he would be able to laugh again, one day . . . or even smile. Mullins took out a pipe and pouch, filled the pipe very slowly and deliberately, fished in his pocket for matches, found them, and lit up, as though performing some old sacrificial rite.

At last he said, 'You know what you'll be in for, I suppose, when you get back to your Section?'

Beck nodded The top-level investigation, the Discipline Form, the hearing, the suspension from duty, the agonising wait for the decision. He had seen it happen to other people, never expected it to happen to him. And the punishment for his own particular breach of conduct would not be just a caution or a fine.

'How many years service?' asked Mullins.

'Twenty-three.'

Mullins puffed on his pipe. 'No previous offences against discipline?'

'No.'

'It's a pity,' said the Inspector solemnly, 'you behaved as you did when O'Ferrall brought you in.'

Beck thought wildly. What had he done? Raved, attacked somebody else? Was his memory wrong?

'Behaved so well,' elucidated Mullins. He was far from being sadistic, but now and then he enjoyed a game of cat and mouse. 'They don't expect passive obedience and knowledge of police procedure from a violent character.'

Beck shrugged 'I just behaved as normal, sir.'

'Ah, that was a mistake. Try throwing your weight about a bit next time. The leopard can't change his spots, remember, or the copper his ways – not after twenty-three years. Never mind. I have your charge sheet here . . . statement made by prisoner . . . police evidence . . . evidence of independent witnesses . . .' He pushed it across the table. 'You know, of course, this will be forwarded to the magistrates' court, who will duly summon you to appear, providing that the object of the assault wishes to prefer a charge.'

'He'll do that, all right,' said Beck glumly. The constable put his head round the door.

'Mrs Beck's here, sir.'

'Keep her outside for a minute. Now, Sergeant, I have to say this to you. I can't see any reason why this incident should make waves beyond – let's say – the Irish Sea, unless you let it. I should talk nicely to your wife, ask her not to spread it around, unless she already has. Am I making sense?'

Beck, scarcely believing his ears, said, 'Yes, sir.'

Mullins smiled, for the first time. 'I'm in your corner, Sergeant.' He dropped one eyelid in a prodigious wink.

'Thank you, sir.'

Marcia and he sat facing each other, cups of tea in front of them. She looked different this morning, pale, as though she hadn't slept, and her make-up was slapdash. He tried to work out ways of saying to her what it had been hinted to him to say, but the words didn't come easily.

'How is he?'

'They discharged him this morning.'

'I know.'

'He's got a headache and a bruise, that's all.' She produced cigarettes and fiddled nervously with the packet. 'And a filthy temper with it. He came straight round and pitched into me, called me all sorts of names.'

'What the hell for?'

'*I* don't know, do I? A lot of stuff about letting someone like you go on seeing me, saying if it was going to be like that he was pulling out. Said he'd thought he was doing the right thing, but he'd changed his mind . . .' She leaned forward. 'Joe, he was scared.'

'Scared?'

47

'Of you. He's afraid you'll keep turning up and the same thing'll happen again.'

'Oh. So where is he now?'

'Gone back to Cushendall.'

'Going to prefer a charge against me, is he?'

'He didn't say. I don't think so. He . . . it's funny, but I think there's something else. When we were having this row he said something about you getting him into trouble, having him investigated, and him not wanting the police nosing about his affairs. What do you think that was about?'

'Did you tell me last night he was in insurance?'

'That's right.'

'Ah.' Fiddles. Something about O'Gorman that had reminded him of a forgery case he'd once handled. Or it could be the dogs, something fishy about placing bets. He drew a deep breath.

'Right, then. Listen. If this – me being in the Nick here – gets back to Hartley, it'll be the finish of me. Out. Discredited copper with no job. No pay. Nothing extra to send you and Carol. So, have you talked?'

'Told anyone? No, there's not been time, since the phone call last night. I said something to mum and dad, but they can't stand Denis and they won't tell, if I ask them. You mean we could keep it quiet?'

'Could be. With an effort.'

Her eyes were large and liquid and appealing, as he remembered them from a long time back; he tried to read the message they were sending him. But it had to be spoken. She said, 'I know it's wrong to say, but you're twice the man he is, Joe. Going for him like that. I knew you were dead against him when I first told you, and it's not surprising, really. But I didn't think you'd go for him like that, for me.'

Not for the first time that morning Beck thought he was dreaming. Marcia thought he'd punched O'Gorman for her sake, because the man was taking over his one-time wife, when it was for Carol, only Carol, to save her; save my darling from the power of the dog. He opened his mouth to tell Marcia so, and then the angel, or whatever it was had moved into the Nick with him, laid a feather of its wings over his lips and cautioned him not to speak. Let her believe she had been fought for.

He allowed himself to say, 'I thought you were all over him last night.'

'Perhaps I was. Perhaps I wanted you to see I could get another feller, a younger man.' She reached across the table and put her hand on his, her small useless pretty hand with its slightly chipped nail varnish. He held it gently, sorry and touched and wary all at the same time, hearing her say, 'I always went for your strength, Joe. You were such a strong man. You still are.'

'Marcia . . .'

'All right. I wouldn't want you back. Or you me. It's just that . . . I'm sorry it's turned out as it has.'

He said, carefully, 'Carol. She's going to be all right?'

''Course she is. She hardly got to know Denis.'

Beck noted the finality of the past tense. 'You don't think he'll be back?'

'No, I don't. He was scared, I tell you. As if I cared — there'll be another along.'

And I'll be on watch for whoever it is, Beck thought.

At the door she said, wistfully, 'I did like that flat, though. I'm sorry about that. 'Bye, Joe. See you when they let you out.'

As the boat for England swayed at its Belfast moorings, the engines throbbing, Beck looked back to where, beyond the quay, beyond the city, in the hills of the north, Carol was. A band of Salvation Army singers and instrumentalists was performing for the benefit of the passengers: or the benefit of their souls, perhaps. The hymn they had chosen was not calculated to raise the spirits of anyone embarking on a voyage.

> The billows swell, the winds are high,
> Clouds overcast the wintry sky;
> Out of the depths to Thee we call;
> Our fears are great, our strength is small.

O Lord, the pilot's part perform,
And guide and guard us through the storm,
Defend us from each threatening ill,
Control the waves, say, 'Peace, be still!'

Perhaps the Sally Army had heard the weather forecast, for the night was savage and black, winds tearing at the boat, waves tossing it like a little car on the Morecambe fairground switchback. Beck drank heavily in the saloon, and then was desperately sick.

'You've lost weight, Joseph,' Jean said, eyeing him thoughtfully.

'Is that all you can say, Ma'am?' He had just poured out to her the whole story of his Antrim experiences, determined to spare himself nothing.

'It's all I'm prepared to say, yes. You've been worrying – don't. No point in it. And you didn't have to tell me.'

'I did, Ma'am.'

'Well. Nobody's ever going to mention it again, unless your friend Inspector Mullins talks in his sleep. At least we know where we are now.'

'Ma'am?'

She was smiling. 'We know we've got a desperate villain on the strength. Who'd have thought it of you, Joseph? Come on, I'll buy you a drink.'

He shuddered. 'I'd rather not, if it's all the same.'

'Have it your way. Oh, and Joseph –'

He paused at the door.

'Thank you. For telling me.'

5 Cause for Complaint

So it was all behind him, and he could settle down again. Never had routine seemed so pleasant, after the prospect which had been before him so recently.

This particular morning routine meant a very small, pathetic puppy, a mongrel with nothing much to it beyond a pair of appealing brown eyes. Beck was nursing it, tickling the neck round which a piece of string was tied. His tone, as he addressed it, was affectionately playful.

'Lost, are we then, Fang? Come to recruit into Police Dog Section? You'll have to take examinations, you know – got to be a very bright dog to join Dog Section, oh yes. And you're such a little chap, too. I'll tell you what – we'll give you a big breakfast first, then we'll take your measurements – see if you're up to standard. Can't promise anything, but I could put in a good word for you . . .'

He hadn't heard the door, but a quiet laugh behind him made him turn, to see Jean. He almost blushed.

''Morning, Ma'am. Er – just checking the stray dogs.'

'So I see . . . hear. Doctor Doolittle lives and can be found in Hartley Police Station. Good morning, Joseph. Any other prisoners?'

'No, Ma'am, very quiet. I've got a couple of lads keeping observations for that flasher. That's all.'

'Good. What do we know about "Hartley Cabs", Joseph?'

'Hartley Cabs, Orchard Street? Bit of a rag-time outfit. Boss, Bill Enstone. Started taxiing with a self-drive a few years ago, now has a few drivers working on a self-employed basis. They pay him a few quid a week for the use of office and radio system.'

'Any trouble?'

Beck stroked the puppy, which had now fallen asleep on the desk. 'Nothing much,' he said. 'Usual con. and used vehicle defects — we've had occasional calls to deal with drunken non-paying customers.'

'Well, I've just driven past there, and it looks like a breaker's yard. Cars all over the place — I saw a blind man forced into the road to avoid some parked on the footpath. Take Roland, and have a word with friend Enstone.'

'Such as . . .?'

'Mark his card, tell him if he doesn't tidy up his parking and get his cars off the footpath, we'll give him some attention. By the look of the set-up, they won't survive a visit from the Traffic Department.'

Beck looked dubious. 'He won't like it, Ma'am — considers himself one of the economic arteries of the town, does Enstone.'

'Tell him he's risking a thrombosis. Give him a firm warning — and it's the last. I'll be watching the situation,' Jean said.

In the shoddy little office of Hartley Cabs, converted from a shop to accommodate the business side of the firm, and behind a partition, the drivers' leisure area to wait in for calls, Beck was administering the warning.

'Those cars,' he said, 'they can't stay like that. Looks like the stadium on stock car night. Get them parked properly or there's going to be summonses flying.'

Bill Enstone concealed any resentment he might feel under a mask of irritation. 'Now, now, Mr Beck. The years you've known me — I always respect the law. Surely, you and this officer can see my situation. It's not me, it's drivers. I tell 'em, but they take not a blind bit of notice. What more can I do? Good reliable drivers like I have are hard to find — I can't afford to upset them. They'd all leave, and my business'd go bang overnight.'

Beck was unimpressed. 'Not too interested in all that, Mr Enstone. All we want is that you keep the law.'

Roland Bentley said, 'If you think it'd work better for one of us to talk to your drivers, I'll do it.'

'Well, I'd really appreciate that.' Enstone made his tone as enthusiastic as possible, but his face did not match it, Beck noticed. But he gave Bentley the nod to go ahead. Enstone watched him disappear into the rest area.

'I must say, Sergeant Beck,' he observed, 'you get some right youngsters on the Force these days. You know what they say, when the bobbies start looking young . . . What's this one's name?'

'Bentley.'

'Good lad?'

'We only have good lads.'

The rest area was no longer quiet. Four drivers shot out towards their standing cars. In a moment the air was full of the sounds of engines starting, and the watchers in the office saw the raggedly parked cars manoeuvred hastily into a kind of order. Cohorts of blind men could now have the footpath to themselves. Bentley returned, beaming.

'You shouldn't have any more problems now,' he told Enstone.

'Well, I'm damned. What did you say to them?' Whatever it was, Enstone resented the way this kid in uniform had manipulated his drivers.

But Roland Bentley was blithely unaware of overtones. Very pleased with himself, he reported back before going to superintend the road crossing outside St Andrew's School. He enjoyed the ferrying to and fro of the children, the importance of having everything stop for him while he halted traffic.

His charges were all across except for two small girls, who stopped half-way, giggling, daring each other to tell him what was amusing them.

'Come on, time for school,' he said. One child stopped giggling long enough to say, 'There's a man. Asleep.'

'Over there,' put in the other. 'Up May Street. Lying on the ground.'

They ran off. Bentley, his duty over, went off to investigate whatever they'd seen. Might be a corpse or a mugger's victim. You never knew. He was having a good morning.

His quarry was indicated to him by the shocked stares in the direction of May Street of two elderly women walking together. They paused, looked, and hurried away, as quickly as their legs would carry them. A slurred voice shouted after them.

'Stupid old bitches. Got your eyeful?'

Bentley saw a figure he knew trying unsteadily to prop itself up against a wall. Joe Berry, twenty-two, no job, no fixed address, heading for the D.T.'s and the cemetery if he didn't mend his ways, which he showed no sign of doing. Dirty, ragged, useless. Bentley felt more than usually superior to him this morning. 'Well, well, well,' he called cheerfully, 'started early today, Joe, did we?'

'Mind your own bloody business.'

'Don't make it my business, Joe. Get off home. You're not fit to be on the street.'

'Leave off, pig,' snarled the vagrant. 'I can look after myself.'

Bentley coaxed. 'Get off home nice and quiet before I have to lock you up.'

'You, you lock me up? Is tha' your idea of a joke? It'd take more than you . . .' Berry reeled against the wall, almost falling.

'Last time.' Bentley's tone was stern. 'Get off home – now!'

The two faced each other, Berry staggering, muttering half-coherent words of hatred. Bentley, watching him keenly, ready to move, failed to notice that a car which had emerged from a street behind him had paused, so that the driver might watch the encounter. The driver was Bill Enstone.

With interest, he saw the constable move towards Berry, who turned, tried to run, and reeled into an iron lamp-standard, his face striking against it full on. He crumpled to his knees, his dirty hands coming up over his face, blood coming through the fingers.

The impact and the fall brought an irrepressible grin to Bentley's face. 'Serves you right, Joe,' he said. 'Are you okay?'

The injured man shrugged away from the hand on his shoulder.

'Get off!' he shouted. 'Bastard! Pig! it's your fault. Get off!'

'Here, let's have a look, Joe.' Bentley forced the screening hands down with his black-leather gloved fingers. There was a long ugly gash bleeding freely on the bridge of Berry's nose, and his eyes would obviously turn black. Nothing too serious. Bentley enquired whether Berry wanted a doctor, and received an unprintable reply.

'All right. You go home, then, and sleep it off.' Satisfied that his duty had been done, he turned away. And the car behind him drove away, its driver mulling over what use he could make of the scene.

Leaving the Nick at the end of his shift, Bentley reported to George Parrish, 'Had a bit of a brush with Joe Berry in May Street. Gave me a bit of lip. Left him with a headache that should keep him quiet for a day or two.'

'Oh? What . . .' Parrish began, but Bentley had gone.

In the crowded, popular vault bar of the Green Elm Joe Berry was showing off his wounds. Blood had caked over the gash on his nose and a slighter one on his forehead, and his eyes were beginning to turn a nasty colour. 'Bloody coppers,' he muttered, staring into his glass of beer mixed with brown ale.

There was a murmur of surprise. Berry was known for injuries befalling him during his drunken meanderings, but coppers were something new. A customer asked him, 'What this time? Get locked up?'

'No. Beat me up, the bastard, didn't he?'

Stares. 'Go on,' said the man at the bar.

'Met this copper in May Street. Just punched me in the face. For nothing – nothing!'

Landlord Boot, behind the bar, asked, 'Have you complained? You should. Summat should be done. Worth a few quid in compo, that lot, shouldn't wonder – five or six hundred at least. I was hearing about a fellow the other day who the coppers beat up, and he got that much, and he wasn't even marked. Go for compo.'

Berry looked baffled. 'What you talkin' about?'

'Criminal compensation they call it – pay out like shelling peas. You got to complain first, though.'

Berry brooded. 'You mean, just go to t'Nick and tell 'em about it – that all?'

A customer who had been hidden behind a copy of *Sporting Life* folded it. 'Excuse me, but I couldn't help overhearing your conversation, young man. My, my, those *are* dreadful injuries. Perhaps I could offer you some help or advice,' said Bill Enstone. Berry regarded him through bleared eyes surrounded by deepening hues of green, purple and black.

'What's it to you?'

'Well, as it happens, I'm being bloody harassed by the Law. For years I've done my all for this town, paid my bloody rates, taxes, brought employment to this area, in exchange for which these bastard local cops are always trying to screw me. Can we have a chat? Brown split, is it? And I'll have a scotch and water.'

Over the drinks, Berry supping his suspiciously, Enstone said, 'I wouldn't mind having a go at these bastards, sort of . . . well, through you. I know a very good lawyer. Put it this way – I'm prepared to fund this lawyer pal of mine a few hundred quid to pursue your case for compensation against cops. You get your compensation, I watch 'em squirm.'

Berry looked confused. Even sober, the argument would have been beyond him without a lot more explanation. Which he got.

When he appeared at the Nick he was, if not sober, less drunk than usual, and the eyes were covered by cheap sunglasses. He was accompanied by a thick-set, middle-aged man. Mr Andrews drew his clients from a very doubtful pool, and looked none too respectable himself.

George Parrish looked up from his clip-board. ''Morning, Joe. Not often you call to see us voluntarily.'

'I want to see t' boss,' Berry said. He'd got that much straight at least.

Jean had just reached her office after a sequence of minor misadventures which had made her late. Trying to sort through the contents of her filing basket, she was not pleased to be interrupted.

'Yes, George?'

'Someone at the counter asking to see you Ma'am. Joseph

56

Berry, local yob. Bit of form, but mainly for drink. Says he wants to complain that a bobby's assaulted him. He's got two real black eyes, but it's the solicitor with him I think spells trouble.'

'Assault? By one of ours?'

'They didn't say, Ma'am.'

'I'd better hear what they do have to say. Fetch them in. And George – when you come back, stay with us, please. I might need some corroboration.'

Berry, looking very far from at home in Jean's office, shifted uneasily in the strong light from the window. Andrews' eye was upon him, willing him to say the right thing. Jean smiled at him encouragingly.

'The Sergeant tells me that you wish to make a complaint, Mr Berry?'

He was suspicious. 'You're the boss?'

'I am Inspector Darblay, in charge of Hartley Police Station.'

'Oh. It were one o' your coppers as beat me up, then, and I want some compo.'

'A police officer from Hartley assaulted you? Why do you say that?'

''Cos it's true. Yesterday dinner-time, in May Street.'

'Why do you think that the person who assaulted you was a police officer?'

That was easy. 'He were in uniform, and I know him. It was that Bentley. Punched me in the face, for no reason. You can see what he did.' He removed the sun-glasses. Jean exchanged a look with Parrish.

'I'm sure you realise that this is a very serious allegation, Mr Berry. You do wish me to record this as an official complaint?'

'I want a form so I can claim compo.'

Andrews butted in. 'Inspector, what my friend Mr Berry means is that he wishes to lodge an official complaint, under the provisions of Section 49 of the Police Act, 1964. He is, of course, also seeking financial compensation for his injuries.'

Jean, disliking him, answered, 'I'm sure Mr Berry knows what he wants.'

'Yes, Inspector, that is so, but he may find your officialese a little confusing, albeit unintentionally so.'

Jean thought Berry would find almost anything confusing, from the look of him. She said coldly, 'I rarely experience difficulty in making myself understood, Mr Andrews. Mr Berry, what I propose to do is to record your complaint. I'll submit it to my Chief Constable, who will appoint a senior officer to investigate it fully. I must warn you, however, that should the investigation prove that your allegation is untrue, you could find yourself in serious trouble.'

She produced from her desk the appropriate form, and glanced without enthusiasm at the statement Andrews had prepared for his client and the doctor's report he had obtained, with lurid photographs of the injuries. She asked Berry, 'Are you willing to be examined by a Police Surgeon and to be photographed by a police photographer?'

'Fetch as many doctors and take as many pictures as you like. I shan't change my story.'

'That's not the intention. We just wish to get the facts recorded accurately.'

Berry sneered back, 'And while you're recordin' the facts accurately, your coppers are out there batterin' people all over the town.'

One copper who was not so engaged was Roland Bentley. Off duty, carefree in jeans and bomber jacket, he was looking lovingly over a motor-cycle, a huge, shining, complex beast of a thing, a triumph of Japanese technology. He loved it, he coveted it. And because it had been a lucky day for him so far he was tempted when the salesman, who knew him and had long had his eye on him as a likely customer, begged him to have a trial run on it.

But as a token gesture he said, 'No point, can't afford it on my pay.'

'Come on! You know I'll sort a right price for you, and you can spread it over three years. After the first couple of months you won't even notice the payments.'

Bentley hesitated, longing to say yes. 'I don't know, Harry. It's still got to be found. And then there's tax and insurance.'

'Your wage is regular, isn't it? No redundancy in your firm, eh? And think of the birds you'll pull with it.'

Bentley wasn't interested in birds, only in the marvellous machine. 'I've applied to go on the bikes,' he said, tempting himself.

'Well, there you are, then. What an impression you'll make on the bosses when they see that you've got a bike of your own like this. Remember Jim Alexander? No, he was before your time. He wanted to go on bikes. I sold him one, not as good as that, and in a couple of weeks there he was, full gear, BMW twin, white helmet, the lot.'

'You're not kidding?' The salesman knew he was caught. He promised to get out some figures while his customer took it for a trial run, very properly wearing a borrowed crash helmet.

When he got back he was glowing with excitement. 'Magic!' he said, and signed on the dotted line where indicated. On the great machine he felt powerful, splendid, in the clouds up above the petty restrictions of everyday life. Not Roland Bentley, but a Speed King . . .

In Jean's office next morning Joseph Berry also signed on the dotted line, though barely able to write more than his name or to read at all. He was puzzled that after all this nobody had yet offered him his compo. money. But Andrews had assured him that it would come, if he made quite sure that he, Andrews, was always present at any interviews or interrogations. Jean shook her head over the document she felt very strongly to be rigged. 'What do you make of it, George?' she asked Parrish, when they had left.

'Berry's a nomark. But Andrews, he's bad news. Villainous lawyer, office in Burnley.'

'See if you can find out more about him. I intend to include some background on Mr Andrews in my report. Is Roland about?'

'He's taken time off this morning. Said he had to see his bank manager or something. He'll be in at eleven.'

'I want to see him as soon as he arrives, please. And I'd better put the Chief Superintendent in the picture. Off the record, George, what do you think? Is Roland in the clear?'

'Bentley wouldn't do anything like this, Ma'am. He's not stupid, and he's not quick-tempered. In fact, he's not quick anything.'

Jean picked up the telephone. 'We need this like a hole in the head. It'll serve as an excuse for all sorts of ferreting into the way the Section's run.'

Roland Bentley roared up to the Nick on the gleaming monster that was now miraculously his – even if the very special price the salesman had mentioned still seemed pretty steep. He ran in, crying excitedly, 'Hey, Sarge, come outside a minute and see what I've bought.'

But Parrish didn't respond. 'The Inspector wants you, right away, Roland.'

'But I'm not due on for nearly ten minutes. Sarge, come and look!'

Parrish continued to write. 'Busy just now,' he said without looking up. 'Go see Inspector. And get properly dressed first.'

Jean, too, didn't respond brightly to his cheerful greeting. Why was everybody so serious today, except him?

'Sit down, Roland. I've just had Joseph Berry to see me.'

'Oh, yes, Ma'am. I bet he's got two lovely black eyes, hasn't he?'

Why did she look at him oddly, and sound surprised as she said, 'Yes, he has.'

'Thought he would, after that do in May Street. Might cut down a bit on the booze now, but I doubt it . . .'

'Berry has made a formal complaint of assault against you. I have recorded the complaint. In fairness I'm telling you that it will be reported and there will be an investigation.'

'Assault?' He laughed incredulously. 'That's rubbish, Ma'am. He walked into a lamp-post.'

'He says you punched him in the face.'

Bentley wasn't laughing now. 'Then he's telling lies. That's all there is to it. I didn't touch him – well, I didn't hit him.'

Jean sighed. She believed him, and she hadn't believed Berry and Andrews. 'You understand I can't talk to you

60

about this? We have to leave it at that. But whoever is appointed Investigating Officer will be wanting to see you.'

She saw Bentley's face change. This was not some kind of joke, but a very real, frightening threat. The thought of his precious new acquisition was crowded out of his mind. And the day had started so well . . .

The Investigating Officer appointed to look into the case was Detective Superintendent Nuttall of H.Q. He was a man with many years of service behind him who believed in discipline, and didn't believe in the appointment of women as Inspectors. As he read the file on the Berry case he felt more and more strongly that the clouting by a copper of a member of the public was the sort of thing he would have expected at Hartley. With the result nicely prejudged in his mind, he went to Hartley accompanied by one Inspector Yates, to whom he had confided his opinion that there was nothing like a bit of fear to tighten discipline, and young Bentley seemed a very expendable character.

He had not met Jean before, which didn't prevent him from using her Christian name at once. One should talk down to women, jolly them along a bit. She disliked him on sight, particularly his smile. But it was important to be civil.

'Not a bad lad, Roland Bentley, sir. Very keen, perhaps a bit slow, but right enough.'

Taking his seat behind her desk, laying papers out on it proprietorially, he smiled again. 'I'm sure, Jean, I'm sure, just a few points to clear up, that's all. Nothing to worry about. A question of satisfying the Director of Public Prosecutions and the Police Complaints Board that everything has been thoroughly investigated and that any wrongdoer has been suitably dealt with.'

'Yes . . . I spoke to Bentley when I got the complaint. He didn't seem worried about it. Said the lad had run into a lamp-post.'

'Let's see if his story stands up under closer examination, shall we? As the saying goes, one tale's good till another tale's told.'

She came back quickly, 'That applies equally to Berry, I would think.'

Nuttall was busy with papers. 'Well, off you go, Jean. I assume you've got a hubby waiting for his tea. I'll be in touch.'

Jean glared at his bent head. 'My husband's used to the erratic hours and meal-times of an *operational* officer, sir. Perhaps I should wait until you've seen Bentley.'

'No need, Jean, no need. Nothing for you to worry your pretty head about.'

If there was one way not to talk to Inspector Darblay, that was it. Furious, only holding on to her control with an effort, she strode out of the room. Furious with Nuttall, anxious for Bentley in the hands of such a man. It seemed ironic that Beck should have got off on a similar charge because of the humanity and understanding of a superior officer. She hoped that Roland might be so lucky, but it seemed unlikely.

When she had left the office Yates said, 'Sensitive, eh, boss?'

'Right. Obviously she wouldn't see anything wrong in her men if she caught them with their pockets full of canteen cutlery. Let's hope it's not going to be a cover-up by the whole section.'

Unlike Jean, Bentley was fooled by Nuttall's wide smile and cordial greeting. He took his seat with confidence, and read without too much attention the form handed to him.

'As you see,' Nuttall said, 'it's a formal notice of complaint that you assaulted Joseph Berry, as provided for by Section 49 of the Police Act, 1964. You'll see that you're not obliged to say anything unless you wish to do so, and whatever you say will be written down and may be given in evidence. But you know all that, and that you can have a Police Federation representative with you during the interview if you want. But you don't have to. I'm sure that we can sort this out without that sort of interference, eh?'

Bentley was puzzled and confused. None of this sounded like just dealing with formalities, as Nuttall had said it would be. He answered nervously the questions that were put to him: his name, his two years in the service, the fact that his father had died when he was four and that he lived with his mother – why did the man want to know such things? He

62

interrupted. 'Don't you want to talk to me about what happened with Joe Berry, sir?'

'In good time. I like to know what sort of lad I'm talking to, first. I like you, Roland, you seem a good sensible copper. I think we understand each other – can be straight with each other, eh?'

'Yes, sir.'

Nuttall barked suddenly, 'Where are your gloves, Roland?'

'Gloves, sir?'

'Gloves. Black leather gloves.'

'In me pocket, sir.' He produced them and Nuttall inspected them, passing them to Yates for checking. Then he asked, mild now, 'How do you think I knew to ask for your gloves, Roland?'

'Don't know, sir.'

'There you are, Roland. You don't know. There's a lot I know that you don't, a lot.You see, Berry told me in his statement that you were wearing black leather gloves. Your gloves have bloodstains on them. Now, Roland, do you want to tell me what *really* happened in May Street?.

Bentley could only say, numbly, 'He ran into a lamp-post, sir.'

'Ran into a lamp-post, Roland? In broad daylight? Come on, that won't do.' Nuttall glanced at Yates, who nodded.

'He *did*, sir. He was very drunk. He could hardly stand.'

'That drunk, was he?'

'He was, sir, shouting and bawling too. Shouted abuse at two women.'

Nuttall put down his pen. 'These two women, they saw all this?'

'I don't know what they saw, sir. But they saw how drunk he was.'

'Who are these women?'

'I don't know, sir. They were passing.'

'H'm. That's a pity. They'd have been a real help.'

Bentley tried to escape. 'Well, he was drunk and he ran into a lamp-post. That's all, isn't it?'

Nuttall leaned forward confidentially. 'I'm afraid not,

Roland. We have to have the full story. We know he was drunk, very drunk, shouting abuse at passing ladies, and he was punched in the face . . .'

'No, sir, it was the lamp-post, he ran into it.' Bentley, never ruddy-faced, was very pale now.

'The blood on your gloves?' Nuttall was purring. 'It won't do, Roland, will it. I'm sure you don't expect Mr Yates and me to believe this, do you?'

'It's true, sir. Honest.'

The desperate plea fell on deaf ears. Nuttall launched into a neatly prepared inquisition on the powers of a police officer. Had it not been Bentley's duty, as such, to arrest a man who was drunk and disorderly, so drunk as he was incapable of taking care of himself? Miserably, Bentley agreed that it had.

'And would you agree that unless this hypothetical police officer was just due to go off duty and didn't want to be delayed by getting involved – then he might deal with it in a totally different way – summary justice? Now, isn't that what really happened? Berry gave you a bit of lip, and you thought you'd teach him a lesson. So you hit him, didn't you, Roland?'

'I didn't, sir. I didn't. Please believe me.'

'What will you say when the lab identifies Berry's blood on these then?' He held up the gloves.

'I went to him, after he'd fallen down, to see if he was badly hurt. He said he wasn't. I must have got it on them then.'

Nuttall's face changed, became ugly. He had been hoping to force out an admission. He got to his feet.

'You think you're a smart ass, don't you, sonny. Think you can kick the system. You'll learn, by God, you'll learn to your cost. But don't come whining to me for help then. I'm finished with you. People like you don't belong in my Police Service, and I'm going to do everything I can to get rid of you.'

The terrible interview was over. Bentley had no doubt of the outcome. Beck, pitying, sympathising with him all too keenly, heard the boy's account of it. At the end he said, 'If you're in the clear, they can't touch you.'

Bentley flashed out, 'If! If! *You*'re the same as *them*! You don't believe me either.'

'Now, Roland, don't get so worked up. Of course . . .'

'I *am* worked up! Too right I'm worked up. Everybody listens to Berry and believes him, gospel. Nobody believes me. Well, you can all get stuffed.'

He had gone, the door slammed behind him.

Joseph Berry cowered against the wall of a disused, half-ruined warehouse. The headlamp of a motorcycle illuminated his terrified face. Bentley was sitting on the machine, helmeted and menacing. He had pursued Berry on it from the pub where he had spent the evening getting into his normal state of drunkenness, across a long tract of waste ground, the hunted man staggering and stumbling, somehow managing to keep his feet, glancing back in terror at the roaring monster behind him. Now he was trapped, the bike and its rider between him and freedom.

'All right, you bastard,' Bentley said. 'You want compensation, do you? Let me sort you out so you can put in a *real* claim for *real* damages.'

Berry put his hands up to guard his face, though no blow had been threatened. 'Get off! Get off!'

'I haven't touched you, yet. That's coming.' The bike moved a little nearer. 'Did you think you were going to get away with it? That you'd get me busted out of my job, ruin my life, with your filthy lies? Didn't you realise one night in some street, I'd be waiting, and nothing, no compensation you got, would pay for the compensation I'd want out of your hide?'

Berry flattened himself against the wall. His knees were shaking.

Bentley's colleagues would not have recognised the voice in which he said, 'This is the end of the road for you, Berry. I'm going to give you five seconds to decide where you end up tonight. Make the choice quick! In five seconds you're going to be on the way to Hartley General Hospital, or on the way to the Nick with me, to make a statement about your lies.

Okay, which is it? Do I break every bone in your body, or is it the Nick?"

Berry gasped out, 'The Nick.'

Jean looked, uncomprehendingly, at the typed sheet in her hand.

'Resignation. Is this a joke, Roland?'

'No, Ma'am, it's no joke. I'm resigning.' His face was set in grim lines.

'Come off it, Roland. It's all over, you're in the clear. Here, I'll forget I've seen this. You'll get over it in a day or two.' She put the paper into his hand, but he refused it.

'No, Ma'am. Most of my uniform's outside. I'll bring the rest in later. My outstanding leave and compensatory time off will more than cover my notice. That's it.'

'That's not it, Roland, far from it. Sit down. What is it that's upset you?'

'The downright injustice of the whole issue. Even villains are presumed innocent until they're proved guilty. I was guilty from the beginning. They talked to me like I was rubbish, told me I was lying, didn't want to hear . . .'

'It came out right in the end, though, didn't it?' She saw his grievance all too clearly, but there had to be a way of getting to him.

'It came out right,' he said savagely. 'because I joined the ranks of the bloody villains, and did what they do – threatened Berry with putting him in hospital. Though of course I don't mention *that* in my report. I always wanted to be a copper, since being little. And I've loved it, all of it, proud to be in it. Perhaps I'm not the best copper there's ever been, but I've tried, tried real hard. And I've never intentionally done anything to let the job down, particularly to let *you* down. I respect *you*, Ma'am, and I wanted to do a right job. But I can't, when my whole future depends on the word of rubbish like Berry. I can't do it, Ma'am. I'm going. My mind's made up.'

It was the longest speech she had ever heard him make, and she knew that he meant every bitter word of it. When he stood up and offered his hand, she took it and held it, seeing tears fill his eyes and feeling them prickling in her own.

'I'll be all right,' he got out. 'Thank you, Ma'am. For everything.'

When he had gone she went to the window, seeing the car park through a misty blur. The beautiful bike was not there: at that moment the salesman was flogging it to someone else, at a very special price.

6 Squirrels and Hoards

Jean turned over in bed, unpleasantly aware that she was awake before she should have been. She pressed the tiny knob on her digital watch that lit up the dial. Five-thirty a.m. What a horrible time to be conscious. She could have slept almost two hours more, and now there'd be no further sleep; she recognised the wide-awake feeling.

Only the faintest, greyest light came through the curtained windows. Outside there was quiet, a faint hum of early traffic from the main road, a car going by. Who drove at this hour? A doctor, going to an urgent case? One of her own patrol cars, scouting?

Tom turned over. She knew now that she had been aware of him tossing restlessly. They had sat up late last night talking endlessly about the crisis he was going through in his Social Services work; a conflict between his own sense of duty and his loyalties towards a friend who had been treated unfairly. She knew too well how Tom felt, much as she herself felt about Roland Bentley, bulldozed out of his career by the inhuman Nuttall. You couldn't have a spate of resignations following on the first one, but she had felt very like it, after Roland had left. And Tom had never been really happy and settled in the work he'd chosen.

He put out a hand and touched her shoulder.

'Awake?'

'Yes. But I didn't want to disturb you.'

'I'm disturbed already. One of those nights.'

He put his arm round her and she cuddled up to him, comforted by his warmth. 'I wonder,' she said drowsily, 'where people go at this time.'

'What people?'

'People in cars. I was listening to them.'

'You ought to know. Could be going anywhere. Your men have got to be on duty by six, haven't they?'

'Mm. And the villains are packing up after a night of looting . . .'

Tom said, 'Fancy an early cup? I'll go down and make one if you like.'

'Thanks, love, I would.'

By the time he came back with it she was asleep again, the long lashes lying on cheeks that were faintly flushed, the short brown hair tumbled on the pillow like a child's. Tom felt reluctant to wake her. Her days were so packed and stressful, she needed every moment of sleep. But the spoon clinked against the saucer, and she woke and smiled at him with her eyes.

Down in Castle Street, Hartley, the traffic had started only fitfully. The drab Victorian terraced houses, some painted in bright incongruous colours by tenants who pined for their native sun, slept in greyness. Even early sparrows didn't bother to haunt Castle Street, preferring the open expanse of the football stadium near by. No life moved in the street; only a cat, locked out the previous night, waited on a step to be let in.

Then a car roared round the corner and drew up outside number 15 with a banging of doors. Four men got out of it. They ran up the steps, hammered with the iron knocker, pressed a bell which failed to work, and shouted, 'Open up!'

The street awoke to their violence. Doors opened, windows went up, voices protested and demanded. At number 15 the clamour brought to the door a young man, naked beneath the coat he had hastily dragged round him. Darren Blake's eyes were heavy with sleep, his face darkly unshaven. Before he could get out a question the men were past him, bursting through a door on the right of the passage. A loud scream came from beyond it.

'Here! You've got no right . . .' He hurried after them into the room. Once a Victorian front parlour, it had been divided by a curtain to make living and sleeping accom-

69

modation. The furniture was makeshift, the decoration, such as it was, patently D.I.Y. In the large low bed behind the curtain, little more than a mattress laid on blocks, a girl was sitting up, clutching the bedclothes round her, her eyes wide and terrified, her long blonde-dyed hair loose on her shoulders. As the four men rushed in she screamed again.

The young man went to her and stood protectively in front of her, too terrified now to speak, gulping with fear.

'I'm Detective Sergeant Winstanley,' said the most senior of the invaders, 'Drugs Squad. We have reason to believe a quantity of heroin is being concealed on the premises.' He produced his warrant card and a form. 'This is a search-warrant. Right, get on with it. Melchett and Daniels, you take the front half of the room. Davies, you deal with this lot. I'll have to ask you to get dressed, madam – and you.' He nodded towards Darren, shivering from the cold and fright.

'I'm not gettin' dressed in front of you!' cried the girl, clutching at Darren's hand.

'We'll leave you to it for a few minutes,' Winstanley said. 'Quick about it, though.' He gestured to the others to follow him through the curtain. In the living-quarters the three constables began to search. The contents of a chest of drawers were tipped out on the floor, a hanging wardrobe investigated, every garment in it turned inside out, the walls tapped.

'What about the fireplace? Shall we knock in this hard-board, sir?' Davies asked, indicating the old boarded-up grate.

'I don't have to tell you everything, do I? Get on with it. All right, are you ready in there?'

The curtain was pushed aside. Darren Blake had got himself into jeans, a shirt and jacket, the girl was in a baggy caftan, a coat round her shoulders. Darren had his arm round her, holding her to him.

'What the hell's all this?' he asked. 'We haven't got no heroin here. Who told you? Why us?'

'You'll be told,' Winstanley snapped. He relied as much on shock tactics as on his men's investigative skill. 'The sooner you help us to find the stuff the sooner we'll be through.'

'He's told you we don't know nothing about no drugs!' the girl shrilled. 'It's not right, you fuzz breakin' into people's homes, frightening us like this!'

'Shut up,' Winstanley said.

'Don't you talk to my wife like that!' Darren tried to look dangerous.

Winstanley smiled. 'Wife? Common-law, I believe.'

The girl started to cry, the boy patting her shoulders, trying to soothe her. 'I'm scared,' she was saying, 'I'm scared, Darren.'

'It's all right, Sue, I won't let them touch you.'

Young Constable Davies said quietly to Winstanley 'Sir. There's something . . .'

Winstanley was turning out a suitcase. 'Where? What have you spotted?'

'Well, sir, perhaps you should ask for a W.P.C. . .'

Melchett appeared and murmured to Winstanley. 'I think you'd get on better without these two, sir. I could get on with questioning them at the Nick while you take the place to pieces. Difficult customers.'

Winstanley nodded, and said to the couple, 'Right, you two. You're going with Detective Sergeant Melchett. And no trouble out of you, mind.'

The two looked unlikely to give trouble. Melchett ushered them towards the door, wishing that his colleague would use a lighter hand with such pitiable creatures. But the tip-off had been strong, from a reliable source.

Outside a crowd had gathered, watching the house, eager for sensation. Winstanley glanced through the front window. Just curiosity-mongers, but there was always a chance of somebody starting something; the police were not popular visitors to Castle Street. But there was only sympathetic crowding as Melchett ushered his captives into the waiting car. As the girl turned sideways, Winstanley saw that she was heavily pregnant. He whipped round to Davies.

'That woman's . . . why didn't you tell me?'

'I tried to, sir.'

Winstanley made a sound something between a bark and a growl. 'Get on, then,' he said.

'We've covered most of the ground in here, except for taking the bed apart.'

'Do it, then. Anywhere else belong to these people?'

'There's her father. Got a room upstairs, the brief says.'

'Must be stone-deaf. Go and look.'

'Yes, sir.'

Jean was putting the final touches to her face when Parrish appeared. 'Mr Davies is waiting, Ma'am, says he must see you.'

'Which Mr Davies? I can think of about twenty.'

'Grocer, Market Street.'

'Oh, the butter-and-egg man.' She knew Mr Evan Davies as one of the few survivals of those Welsh traders who had come from the dairy-farms of Wales during the nineteenth century to prosper in the supplying of milk, butter, eggs and cheese to the towns and cities of England. Roberts, Davies, Lloyd, Evans, Jones, there had been one in most streets, until the big milk distributors and the supermarkets had driven them out. This particular Davies had somehow survived by adding other goods to his dairy products and keeping a consistently high standard. Jean patronised him for good cheeses and hand-cut bacon and hams, and the home-made quiches his wife turned out, quite unlike anything from a delicatessen fridge.

'Wheel him in,' she said. 'I hope he's handing out free samples.'

Evan Davies was the archetypal Welshman of farce, small, perky and puckish, his accent as powerful as his strongest cheese. He had never been a nuisance, only calling the police in once after an attempt on the part of hopeful youths to break down his solid Victorian shutters, still put up every night, as they had been by himself and his predecessors for a hundred years.

He bustled in, smiling, bright-eyed. 'Good morning, Inspector, a nice day, isn't it. I hope I see you well.'

'Reasonably, thank you, Mr Davies. That was a fine batch of bacon you sold me last week. Keep me some more if you've got any.'

72

'I will indeed, Inspector. There's good of you to say so, and Mrs Davies would like you to know she's working on a new spinach flan.'

'I'll look forward to that. What's the trouble, if any?'

He fished in a pocket. 'Well, now, it's these. One last week, and another yesterday. I didn't notice at the time, don't ask me why, unless it's my glasses need changing. I'd like to know what you think.' He handed over two round pieces of metal, neither polished nor quite dull, uneven of surface.

'Counters?' Jean guessed. 'Tokens?'

'I thought of that, Ma'am, and then it seemed to me they would be foreign currency. You know how it is, they bring it back and try to pass it off.'

Jean switched on her desk-lamp and examined them, then took them to the window. She turned back to Mr Davies.

'Any idea who passed these particular ones on to you?'

'That I don't know, Inspector. But I should say kids, we get a lot of them shopping for their mothers. The teenagers, now, they don't come in much, prefer the synthetics, they do – bubblegum, you know, that sort of thing.'

'They would. Well, I'm not sure what we've got here, Mr Davies, but we'll ask round and see if anyone else is getting them. Will you watch any money you take very carefully, and make a note of any more that come in, and who tenders them?'

She instructed Parrish to include milk roundsmen and newspaper sellers among persons questioned. He tried to stifle a yawn; not so much because the enquiry was a boring one, but he had been up half the night with his youngest child who had earache, and had then to go on duty for six a.m. It had been no help to have Ma'am arriving almost two hours earlier than usual; she'd been awake early and wanted to catch up with arrears of work. She might be bright-eyed and bushy-tailed first thing in the morning, Parrish thought, but he certainly wasn't.

As he half-dozed over his day-book the door opened. Melchett propelled in his charges from Castle Street. He was as white-faced as Darren Blake, half-carrying the girl Sue.

73

'George, do something, for God's sake! I'd no idea — it came on in the car — I stopped, but . . .'

Parrish took one look at Sue and bolted to Jean's door.

'Ma'am, quick, please. There's a young woman . . . I think she's in a bad way.'

Jean wasn't prepared for the particular bad way Sue Blake was in.

'What have you brought her here for?' she snapped at Melchett. 'Couldn't you see she's a hospital case?'

Melchett began to stammer. Jean remembered that he hadn't been married much above a year and certainly had no experience of fatherhood. Tough CID man he might be, but he looked in almost as bad a state as the boy who was saying, over and over again, 'Help her, help her! you've got to help her! *Do* something!'

Jean said, 'George, you and I are going to manage this. Help me get her into the rest room, then telephone for the ambulance and put the kettle on, in that order. Come on, love, you're going to be all right. Sergeant, look after that young man, and keep the explanations for afterwards.' She hoisted up the moaning, gasping girl, and with Parrish on the other side propelled her down the corridor to the small, hardly-used room reserved officially for anyone ill or faint. For the first time in its life it was to be pressed into service as a maternity ward.

An hour later she returned to the desk, where Beck, hurriedly summoned, was on duty. He barely raised an eyebrow at the dishevelled apparition of his Inspector, a bloodstained cleaner's overall covering most of her, her sleeves rolled up and her face shiny with exertion.

'Well, that's it, Joseph. Another satisfied customer, or rather two, if you count one healthy boy, weight unknown, still a bit moody from the quick trip.'

'Well done, Ma'am. The ambulance is on its way.'

'Why wasn't it here an hour ago?'

'Some sort of hold-up.'

'I see,' said Jean grimly. 'One of those mornings. When they've collected the patient I want to see Sergeant Melchett and anybody else responsible for that girl being frightened into labour and brought here without me being consulted. It just happens that I'm handy at first aid. Suppose I hadn't been?'

Beck shook his head. 'Rather you than me.'

She looked round. 'Where's the husband?'

'Canteen. On his eighth coffee. And talking about damages . . .'

'I see. Get me Chief Inspector Wigan. Now.'

The unforgettable morning was over, the rest room restored to something like its normal condition, Jean cleaned up but still smouldering with rage at the CID's crass idiocy in landing their mistakes on her. The whole operation had been a kingsized mistake, for after all that no sign of drugs had been found at the flat in Castle Street.

She was working off her feelings in a written complaint when Beck came in. 'Davies the shop called again. More tokens in the till, and he's identified the culprit.'

'*Has* he.' She was still writing.

'Small boy from Waterloo Estate. He palmed off several this time, getting cheeky, and Davies spotted them, but the lad ran off. Tommy Dawson, 64 Waterloo, ground floor. Want to see them, Ma'am?'

'No, haven't time. Get Constable Moss to go round there and look into it. Tell him to wait till school's out.'

PC Ronald Moss knocked at the door of the flat: one of those front doors with glass at the top and little draped curtains behind it. The young woman who answered gave the usual frightened start at the sight of his uniform.

'Yes? What is it?'

Moss had a reassuring smile. 'Not bad news or anything. Mrs Dawson, is it?'

'That's right.'

'Is your Tommy at home?'

'He's having his tea. He hasn't done nothing, has he?'

'Can I come in?' Gently he made it impossible for her to shut the door against him. The small untidy woman was matched by the small untidy living-room. On the littered table, roughly set for tea, a milk-bottle was side by side with a half-wrapped packet of margarine; a baby girl in a high chair was enjoying sole possession of a jar of jam. Tommy Dawson, thin and spectacled, froze at the sight of a policeman, his mouth half-full of currant bun. His mother hovered protectively over him.

'I'd like to talk to Tommy, Mrs Dawson,' Moss said.

'He hasn't done nothing!' She suddenly turned on the boy. *Have* you?'

'No, mum,' Tommy said through the bun.

'Mind if I sit down? It's just this, Tommy. You know Mr Davies, the grocer? You go to his shop for your mum, don't you. Well, it seems like you've been paying him in these.' He held out a handful of the metal objects. Tommy didn't need to examine them, but his mother did, and Moss saw her face clear.

'Them's not real money,' she said. Moss knew that for a bad moment she had thought they were real money, stolen by her son. 'Just some old stuff.'

'Them's real all right,' the boy said. 'I thought it'd save a bit to use 'em – while me dad's skint.'

'Out of work, is he?'

'Been months now,' Mrs Dawson said. 'He got the push from Cateley's and he's never got owt else. But you shouldn't have, Tommy. Where d'you get them?'

'Found 'em. Out there.' He gestured. 'Lots of 'em. I'll show you if you like.' Moss inspired confidence in people, particularly children. He had been the father of a son for exactly one year, and it had done a lot for his attitude to the junior townsfolk of Hartley, trying though they could be at times.

He followed Tommy round the corner of the flats. Behind lay a stretch of undeveloped land overgrown with weeds and scrub and old trees, a haven for birds. Tommy led him to a spot screened by trees from the windows.

'I were trying to make a bit of garden, there.' Moss saw a square of earth roughly turned over and bordered with stones, a few seedlings dying and dead in it.

'You won't grow a lot in that, lad. It wants properly digging and some fertiliser on it.'

'I know. I did try, I went right down, but then me spade broke.' Moss saw the remains of it, the seaside variety that went with a bucket. 'Only I found *them* there. D'you want to see?' Kneeling, he scrabbled in the earth with the spade-handle and pulled up a tin that had once held shortbread. Glancing round to make sure nobody but Moss was watching, he prised it open. 'I put 'em in a tin so's I wouldn't lose any.'

Moss looked down at almost half a tinful of dark things huddled together like sleeping toads. It seemed unlikely that any shopkeeper would have accepted them as legal tender. He said as much.

'They don't look great,' Tommy said, 'but if you polish 'em with Brasso they come up real nice.' He rubbed one on his sleeve. Moss looked, then stared. 'Aye, they do,' he said.

Tommy was still waiting for a telling-off. 'I shouldn't've give 'em to Mr Davies, should I.' He burgeoned into confession. 'I used some for ticket machines on t'buses, an' all.'

'Well, I wouldn't use any more if I were you. In fact, I'm going to ask you to let me have these to show 'em down at the N . . . police station. We'll look after them for you.'

'Will I get into trouble?'

'No, I shouldn't think so. Only don't spend anything again unless you know the value of it.'

'All right. There's this, too.' He fished out a small, greenish object and put it into Moss's hand.'

'Thanks. Do a lot of digging, do you?'

The boy shrugged. 'Not much else to do round here.' He walked back with Moss to the car, watching his prized tin vanish into the boot with the key turned on it.

Jean spread the coins out over her desk blotting-pad until they covered it. At the Museum they had been thoroughly washed and buffed until they shone with something of their original lustre. From every one looked out the face of a man, curly-haired, curly-bearded, and round the head were letters, worn away, like the face, in some coins, legible in others.

'Roman coins, second century,' Jean said to Moss and

77

Beck. 'The Emperor Septimus Severus, well-known in these parts, it seems. Metal, gold mixed with copper. Value considerable. Plus one earring.' She held it up, a slip of dark jade with a seahorse carved on it, suspended from a thin hook of wire, once the ornament of a Roman lady's ear. 'Pretty, isn't it.'

'But why would such a lot of coins have got left?' Moss asked. 'I mean, altogether like that. You'd think someone would have nicked 'em before now.'

'How do I know? Perhaps the land behind Waterloo Flats used to have a Roman settlement on it, and these were in somebody's cellar. Perhaps they were found a long time after and thrown away again. Somebody ought to put Tommy Dawson up on a bulldozer and get him to turn a few more up.'

'Treasure trove,' Beck mused. 'So there'll be a reward.'

'To the finder if reported promptly. I think we'll regard Tommy's report as prompt, even if it wasn't quite spontaneous. Now these go to the coroner for an inquest.'

'Reminds me of Castle Street,' Beck said idly. The pay-off to the CID's calamitous raid had been that no trace of heroin or any other drug had been found on the premises. But upstairs, in a cubby-hole off the small room where Sue Blake's father lived, they turned up a hoard of another kind. Small shop-lifted objects, or filched from the outside displays of shops, in the main: teacups and dishes and trinkets from the cheap trays of antique shops, kitchen-ware from Asian general-purpose dealers, a holy picture, a garish figurine – imitation Chelsea, a child's pencil-box, a pink cuddly toy. The man, a helpless drop-out, had no explanation to give, and was bound over. There was a strong suspicion in the CID that it had been he, for malicious reasons nobody would ever know, who had given false information to their snout.

'Don't talk to me about Castle Street, Joseph,' Jean said, 'ever again.'

7 Tricks

Constable Farley, on night patrol in Number Two area, was bored. The night was drizzly, a thin drizzle which had something like the effect of steam, blurring outlines and raising a kind of dull shine, like poor boot-polish, on the scenery of the streets. It was, he thought, rather like being part of an old German mono film. Nobody in their right mind would be out in it, and very few were. Farley speculated on what might have brought them out: a visit to an all-night chemist, a return home from late shift? He had been in the Force for five years, the last three in a lively urban area with all sorts of trouble constantly breaking out. Since he had been temporarily posted to Hartley as Roland Bentley's replacement his life had become very dull.

To amuse himself he began to whistle, very softly, all the television theme-tunes he could remember. It would have been entertaining to break into corresponding steps, but he restrained himself and concentrated on any that had words to them. There was the old Z-CARS theme, which had grown out of a Liverpool folk-tune.

> Johnny Todd he took a notion
> For to sail the ocean blue,
> And he left his true lover
> Weeping by the Liverpool sea . . .

It wasn't great poetry, didn't even rhyme, but it gave his mind something to do. He had a shot at more of it.

> I will buy you sheets and blankets,
> I will buy you . . .

The whistling stopped short. About to pass a shop doorway, his eye caught a thin line of light filtering through the door, a crack open. The light flickered – a torch. Upstairs the windows were dark, blank – no resident shopkeeper.

Very quietly, the adrenalin beginning to flow, he pushed the door wider. The beam of the torch was bobbing along one side of the shop, lighting a multiplicity of objects: crockery, kitchen ware, clocks, wristwatch straps, photograph frames, cheap jewellery. Three men with their backs towards him were stuffing them into carrier bags.

'Well, well,' said Farley affably, 'open all hours, this place, is it?'

There was confusion of movement, swearing, clatter. Two of them were past him and through the door before he had time to curse himself for speaking before acting. The second gave him a violent push which almost sent him sprawling, but he kept his balance and grabbed at the third man, who, his hands hampered by the torch and the carrier-bag, wriggled in vain in that experienced hold. Farley kicked the door shut and shone his own torch on his captive's face.

'Now where've I seen you before, son?' he asked, and was answered in lurid language. As the boy struggled, a heap of piled buckets went down with a great clangour, and glass splintered under his threshing feet. Farley spoke into his radio. '7083 to Hartley. Break-in at Slater's Stores, Oldham Street. One thief captured, two on the run. Mobile required.'

Jean, too, recognised the face she saw next morning through the peep-hole of the cell door. It was a striking face, even a beautiful one, by the standards of classical art. Fair skin, a straight Grecian nose, a mouth almost femininely curved, dimpled chin, light waving hair, a strong column of throat. He reclined easily on the bunk like a resting athlete.

'Philip Ormrod,' she said to Beck, 'again. How many times does that make?'

'Lost count, Ma'am. The first year I was here he went to the Detention Centre, and since he came out it's been . . . oh, ten or a dozen times, take or leave.'

She was studying the prisoner. 'Funny, with a face like

that. You'd think he could make a living at something other than burglary.'

'Oh, he's pretty versatile. Common assault, attack on bus inspector, football hooliganism, paternity order . . .'

'At that age? Oh, well.' She went into the cell, Beck behind her.

'Good morning, Philip. You can't keep away from us, it seems.'

The boy's eyes slid over her, slowly. He was reminding himself of her age, attractions, if any, and sexual availability. The eyes were china-blue and completely cold.

'Didn't ask to come in, did I.'

'No, and we didn't ask to have you. It won't just be a caution this time, you know.' Philip's spectacular looks had had their effect on more than one susceptible female magistrate.

He shrugged and rolled over, his back to her. Outside the cell she said to Beck, 'He may be pretty, but there's something absolutely repulsive about him as well. I'd say he's as near as they come to a psychopath.'

Beck was not feeling bright. 'Ma'am?'

'Somebody with no ability to enter into other people's feelings. The sort you wouldn't care to have standing over you with an axe. Dangerous.'

'Shouldn't be surprised. A nasty bit of work.'

The nasty bit of work got off as lightly as he usually did. It was as though his appearance persuaded magistrates and judges, even with the facts before them, that he wasn't as bad as he seemed. His small, cowed-looking mother testified to his being a good lad at heart, easily led astray by evil friends. He was sentenced to a month's work as odd-jobber in a mental hospital; Jean was sorry in advance for the patients.

When, three weeks later, she read in the *Hartley Clarion*, of a series of thefts at the hospital, she made a cynical face. 'Same old story,' she said to Tom. 'They won't believe it's our Philip till they catch him with the stuff falling out of his pockets.' She returned to the local news page.

'What about this, then? Cowley must be running short of copy.'

Tom helped himself to toast. 'Why?'

'They're telling ghost stories now. "The Haunted House in Churchill Street".'

Tom thought. 'Churchill Street's new. Well, post-war. Council houses on an old bomb site. Shouldn't have thought there'd be a lot of haunting round there.'

'Well, there is, according to this. "Family terrified by outbreak of supernatural happenings. Mrs Poley, 51, told our reporter that life at 12 Churchill Street had become impossible because of unexplained noises, particularly at night, objects flung across rooms, and crockery smashed by some unseen agency. 'It is terrible,' she said, 'we have no peace at all, not knowing when the next thing is going to happen. Only this morning another teacup broke. My nerves are in rags and I am under the doctor for it. We are asking the council to rehouse us as soon as possible.' Mr and Mrs Poley have one daughter, Theresa, 16".'

'Delusions. It's not uncommon — women have a run of household breakages and start thinking there's something uncanny about it.'

'Theresa Poley. I know her. At least, I've met her, when I gave the prizes at St Joseph's. She was practically their star pupil — rows of O-Levels and non-stop appearances on the platform to collect prizes for just about everything. Very, very bright. Very pretty, too. A good Catholic girl who won't be taking herself off to a nunnery.'

Tom gave no further thought to Theresa Poley or her mother's household ghost until the telephone call came.

Jim Ferrers of the Housing Department, something of a mate of his, said, 'I don't really want to alert your lot officially, but it's this business in Churchill Street. You may have seen it in the rag.'

'Jean did. The Poley family.'

'That's right. We've had an application from Mrs Poley — several, in fact — for rehousing, and it's not an obvious case. As you know there's not a lot going in the way of alternative accommodation for families without obvious need, and frankly the Poleys don't qualify. Healthy conditions, house only thirty years old or so, no invalids, no neighbour trouble or persistent vandalism. As to this ghost business, well. What do we say? I've asked around and there's a so-called medium, a Mrs Dutton in Hillcrest Road, who reckons she can sort the whole thing out.'

'And . . .?' Tom asked.

'And she's got an appointment to go round there. Sunday afternoon. I was wondering if you'd like to take yourself round as well, and see what you make of it?'

Tom sighed. It sounded like the least promising assignment in a very unpromising period. 'What do you want to know, in particular?'

'Whether things are really going bump in the night, or the day, or whenever. What the Poleys are like, especially Mrs, in the light of your own experience of disturbed people. In fact, I'd rather like you to give us a case for saying that rehousing isn't necessary.'

Jean was intrigued. 'Can I come, too? It sounds a lovely change from flesh-and-blood villains, and it would be my first case of the haunts.'

'With respect, love, it's not your case, and I think me *and* a medium might be enough for the Poleys.'

'Oh well, be like that. I can always get on with the garden. But I'd have enjoyed it . . .'

Tom felt guilty, settling himself into the Poleys' front parlour, a very ordinary room in a very ordinary small house. Jean loved a mystery, and was fascinated by the inexhaustible mystery of human nature. Her bright eyes would have been everywhere, noting significant things about the furniture, the atmosphere, the people. Whereas he, who worked so hard at understanding, could see only that Mrs Poley was too thin and suffering from nervous strain, a woman whose good looks had been lost along the way, though she might once have been very like her daughter Theresa. Theresa was tall, long-legged, slim-waisted and broad-hipped, with large dark eyes in an elfin face and she had brown hair with a natural curl in it. She spoke with a less pronounced accent than her parents, and she was as much on edge as her mother, but in a different way. Tom wished he knew how different, and why. Mr Poley was stocky and as and as ordinary as his house. His blue eyes were choleric and his manner was unwelcoming.

'I didn't ask for you, Mr Whatsyername, but as you're here you'd best come in.'

'Mr Ferrers of Housing thought . . .'

'Aye, well, he may have, but I don't want him or his rehousing. Don't you take notice of my wife, she's at a funny age. Maybe you can talk her out of it.'

His wife, behind him, looked and sounded outraged. 'Dad! What a way to talk. What's Mr Darblay going to think of us?'

'I don't know and I don't care.' He marched before them into the sitting-room and knelt by the television set, unplugging it.

'You're never going to take that through?' Mrs Poley cried.

'Of course he is, mummy.' Theresa tossed her curls. 'He's not going to be done out of a Sunday afternoon's soccer, are you, dad?'

'That I'm not, lass. Kick-off's two-thirty.' He coiled up the lead-wire and pushed the set on its wheeled trolley out of the room. They heard him shut the door of the next room with an ostentatious bang, and the voice of a television announcer soar above the normal level.

'I'm sorry.' Mrs Poley almost wrung her hands. 'He's mad about that football – mad, he is.'

Theresa turned on her. 'Why shouldn't he be? Better than being mad about . . . other things.'

'You be quiet!'

'No I won't, mummy.' The dark eyes sparkled with something Tom thought might be anger. 'Mr Darblay's come to see what we're like, so we'd better let him see, hadn't we.' She bestowed a beautiful smile on him. 'Your wife gave the end-of-term prizes at our school. I think she's smashing.'

'Thank you. So do I. She did mention you – said you were very clever.'

'That she is,' Mrs Poley put in. 'Studying for her A-levels now, and they think she might beat the school records – if she keeps working, not fooling about wasting herself when she ought to be thinking about her career – and you know Miss

Lacey said you could do anything, anything at all you wanted in life, Theresa . . .'

'Jesus, Mary and Joseph!' said the girl so loudly that even the next-door blare of the television was overtopped. 'Will you shut up about my life, mummy, just for once?'

As Mrs Poley burst into tears the front door bell rang.

The new arrival was Mrs Dutton the medium. She was middle-aged, widowed, ultra-respectable, and quietly dressed in a neat suit with a neat blouse and a quite good brooch. Her hair was greying, her make-up minimal. Tom had imagined someone gipsyfied, the sort of Madame Zora who invited you into her kiosk at Blackpool to share her talents with crowned heads of all nations. But Mrs Dutton was pure Women's Institute and took the three of them in with one quick glance: the embarrassed Tom, the weeping mother, the angry girl. She appeared to notice nothing wrong as she said, smiling, 'Well, how nice to be here, and how nice of you to ask me.'

'*I* didn't ask you,' Theresa snapped rudely. The medium seemed not to hear her. 'I've taken the liberty,' she said, 'of getting a friend of mine to come along. He's so very interested in manifestations, and so experienced, I thought he might very well be a help. Bill Righton – the Reverend Bill, you know, from All Angels'.'

'We're Catholics,' Theresa said.

'I know, dear. But that doesn't matter, does it, one little bit. We're all Christians, aren't we, and it's up to us to fight the forces of evil together, if evil is what we're up against here. It may be something quite different, of course. A troubled spirit, perhaps.' The bell rang again. Mrs Dutton glanced through the window. 'Good, he's right on time. I hope his bicycle's going to be all right there. I'll let him in, shall I?'

They heard her cheerful voice at the door before she led in the Reverend Bill, young, plump, spectacled and jolly of face, wearing jeans and a baggy sweater. Tom, who had met and liked him, was relieved to have the support of another man's presence. They shook hands.

'I thought you handled that baby case in my parish very

ably,' the Reverend said. 'Seemed a bit hard, taking the kid into care, but the poor woman obviously couldn't cope in the first place, never had and never would.'

Mrs Poley snapped, 'It's any mother's place to look after her child.'

'Oh yes, indeed, but in those circumstances ... well, it's over now. And how about you, Mrs Poley? You've been having disturbances, Mrs D. tells me?'

'Terrible. I can't begin to tell you, Mr ...er ...'

'Bill, just Bill.'

Mrs Poley, unused to priestly informality, hurried on. 'A fortnight ago, it all started. First it was knockings at night, on the wall just behind our bed. One – two – three. Then a bit of a pause before it started again. One – two – three. Like tapping out a message. Theresa heard it in the next room, didn't you. And next morning the first smash came – a basin slipped off the edge of the draining-board, just like someone was pushing it, and broke to bits on the floor. Since then it's been one thing after another.' She looked nervously round the room. 'And not just breakings, silly sorts of things, like a bag of potato peelings flying across the kitchen – made ever such a mess.'

'Interesting,' Mrs Dutton said. 'Very much the usual poltergeist pattern, wouldn't you say, Bill?'

'Oh, I would. Minor breakages, pointless mischief. They're silly children who only do it to annoy, poltergeists.'

'We don't always know *what* they are, dear, do we. Wandering elementals, non-human, that is, or perhaps influences left over from past ages. I speak at our Spiritualist Church every Sunday, Mrs Poley, and some of the stories I hear are quite remarkable. I'm glad to say that in many cases I've been able to help – sometimes just by visiting the house. For instance, have you noticed how the atmosphere in this room has changed in the last few minutes? There's a kind of stillness –'

They all jumped as a china mug leapt from the end of the mantelpiece and shattered on the fender.

Mrs Poley had gone white, her hands clasped at her throat. Theresa was staring at the remains of the mug. Mrs

Dutton's face beamed with satisfaction. 'There,' she said, 'it's telling us it's present. Perhaps that was a little cry for help. I hope that wasn't a valuable piece, Mrs Poley?'

'It was a Coronation mug. The Queen, 1952. I expect I could get another, somewhere . . .'

'So you're not too disturbed about it. That's quite usual.'

'They don't want to distress you, you see,' Bill Righton clarified, 'just to make you notice them.'

'I've noticed them, all right.' She looked from one to the other. 'You see what it's like, don't you? No peace, day and night – it's driving me mad.'

Bill Righton turned to Theresa, who had seemed the least disturbed by the crash. 'How about you, Theresa? Are you worried by it?'

She shrugged. 'It's a nuisance. The knocking's kept me awake sometimes, but I don't get as much of the rest of it as mummy does – I'm at school or doing outside things most of the time. I keep telling and telling her it'll go away. Can't you exorcise it, Father? Or doesn't your church do that sort of thing?'

He smiled. 'Oh yes, my church certainly does – and more often than you'd think. But I think you'd better ask your own parish priest about that. It seems to me Mrs Dutton's the person to help you, in the first place. What are your impressions, Elsie?'

'I'm not sure. Rather mixed . . . Can we all sit quietly for a few moments?'

They watched her, calm and relaxed in the stiff uncomfortable chair, her palms upturned on her lap, her face serene, listening. Then she asked, 'Is this old ground, where the house stands?'

'It was a bomb site,' Mrs Poley said.

'But before that?'

Theresa volunteered, 'It probably belonged to the Castle – Castle Street's just round the corner, and the Castle was here until Cromwell besieged it. After that there wasn't much left, so they pulled it down and used the stones for building. I know, because we did a project about the history of Hartley before the nineteenth century.'

'So this would be very old dwelling land,' Mrs Dutton said thoughtfully. 'Violence, conflict, quite possibly murder. That might very well account for the troubling here. There's certainly stress, great stress. I feel it in the air, all round me. And I ask myself, why should this echo of old violence, if that's what it is, suddenly break out?'

The clergyman said, 'A focal point, perhaps? Someone being used as a channel? Theresa, how old are you?'

'Sixteen, and two months. What about it?'

'I think I know why you asked that, Bill,' said Mrs Dutton. 'The adolescent in the house. Young energy channelled into manifestations.'

Theresa jumped out of her chair. 'If you're saying it's me doing it, I'm not! What would I want to do anything so stupid for? Of all the daft ideas!'

'Sit down, Theresa.' The medium's voice was gently authoritative. 'We're not saying you yourself are responsible. But it very often happens in cases of this kind that the spirit, or elemental, is making use of the natural energy of a very young person.'

'Like plugging itself into an electric socket,' Bill Righton added.

Theresa looked sullen. 'I don't believe it. Anyway, things happen when I'm out. I'm fed up with all this. If neither of you knows what it's all about, you can't be much good.' She turned on her mother. 'And if you hadn't gone on and on about it, it might all have stopped before this.'

'Don't be so rude!'

Mrs Dutton said calmly, 'Suppose we all stop talking. When the vibrations we're causing have died down, I may be able to get through to this restless person who wants to communicate with us. Very quiet, now.'

Tom, who had kept well out of the discussion, watched the other three. Bill Righton was too full of eagerness to keep eyes or hands still, Theresa's face was set in surly lines, and her mother was as bad a case of nervous stress as he had seen for a long time. When the medium, her eyes closed, began to speak to nothing visible, he was conscious of acute embarrassment.

'Are you with us, friend? We're here to help you. Will you give us a sign of your presence?'

No sign came. Mrs Poley looked wildly around her, as though something might spring up through the floor. Mrs Dutton tried again.

'There is nothing at all to be afraid of. We are all friends. Won't you trust us?'

The door burst open. Mrs Poley shrieked. But it was only her husband who stood there, a picture of pent-up rage.

'What the hell's going on in here? I can't concentrate on me match with a pack of fools on t' other side of wall brewing up witches' spells or whatever it is. Have you found owt, missis? Well, have you?' He cut short Mrs Dutton's attempt to answer. 'No, you've not, and I'll tell you why – because there's nowt here but folk, and it's folk that's been playing tricks.' He rounded on his wife. 'If you've got hold of some joker to make me think this house isn't fit to live in, you can call it off, I'm not moving a step. I don't know which of you it is, you or our Theresa, but if your clever pal keeps up his row I'm off to t' police.' He turned and slammed out of the room.

Mrs Poley began to sob. Mrs Dutton patted her arm.

'Don't upset yourself. Perhaps this wasn't the time to investigate.'

'We'll take ourselves off and leave you in peace,' Bill Righton said, getting up.

Mrs Poley mopped her eyes. 'No, you must have a cup of tea. You can't go without a cup of tea.' She went to the kitchen.

A moment later they heard the crash of crockery.

Tom reported back to Jim Ferrers on Monday morning.

'There's certainly something funny going on there.' He described the breaking of the mug, and subsequent kitchen incident. 'I can't believe it's poltergeists. But it happens. They're all on edge, mother, father, daughter, ready to fly at each other's throats.'

Ferrers sighed. 'So you think there's a case for rehousing?'

'I honestly don't know, Jim. The mother seems to be the only one who wants it. And if they go, who's going to move in after the publicity there's been?'

'That's true. Well, I don't know where we go to from here – unless we turn the application down and offer to reconsider when the ghosts have had time to settle down. Or applied to have themselves rehoused.' He laughed hollowly.

About the time Tom and Ferrers were talking, Sergeant Parrish appeared in Jean's office.

'Young girl to see you, Ma'am. Name of Poley.'

'Poley? Theresa Poley?'

'That's right.'

Jean greeted Theresa with a warm smile. The girl looked in need of reassurance, nervous, uncertain of herself, and very awed by her surroundings.

'Sit down, Theresa. You're an early caller. Shouldn't you be at school?'

Theresa gulped. 'I cut it. Rang up to say I was ill but I'd turn up later. I wanted to see you.'

'So here I am. What's the trouble?'

'Your . . . Mr Darblay told you about yesterday, at our house?'

'Mr Darblay did. It didn't sound like a happy afternoon.'

'It wasn't, it was terrible.' The words were coming with a rush. 'The worst was when dad said he was going to the police. I knew what that was going to mean, people coming and looking everywhere, asking questions . . . it's been bad at home since it started, dad shouting and carrying on, and mummy jumping with nerves. I've not been able to work, not even in my room. I'm going to fail my A-levels at this rate, and I can't stand any more.'

Jean was pretending to make notes. 'Any more of what?'

'All that poltergeist stuff . . . Dad's not been here yet, has he?'

'No. Go on, Theresa.'

'Well, at first I was a bit scared, with all the breakages and the knocking at night. Mummy seemed frightened out of her mind. All the time she was going on at dad about how we'd have to move, phoning the Housing people. She even got a reporter round, to put something in the paper. Dad wouldn't listen – he said it was all a lot of nonsense, though I could see he didn't like it. But he'll never move from that house because it's just round the corner from the football stadium.'

'And you, would you like to move?'

Theresa looked at the carpet. 'No.'

'You'd better tell me about it. That's what you came for, isn't it?'

'Yes, Mrs Darblay. I mean Inspector. You see I found out yesterday. About the poltergeist. I'd half-guessed at times, but I couldn't be sure. After they'd gone, Mrs Dutton and Mr Righton, mummy went to bed because she was upset, and I tidied up the room.'

'And?'

'The mug that fell off the mantelpiece. It had a piece of black thread tied to its handle.'

'Oh.'

'Yes. It was mummy's doing all along. She broke the plate in the kitchen, afterwards, so they'd still think it was going on. She did all the pot-breaking with thread, and the knocks with a stick she kept under the mattress, her side of the bed. She threw the things herself, the potato peelings and once an egg.'

'Yes, I see. It's been done before – I was reading it up last night. So your mother made everyone think the house was haunted. Why, Theresa?'

The girl was calmer now, looking more mature than the troubled child she had been. 'To get us out of the house.'

'That wasn't all, was it.'

'No. To get me away from Phil.'

Facts and images were marshalling themselves in Jean's memory. A series of charge-sheets, an address in Castle Street, a boy with the face of a fallen angel, a break-in that had only led to a probation order.

'That would be Philip Ormrod.'

A warm blush spread over Theresa's face. 'Yes. Phil. Mummy was very upset when he got into a bit of trouble lately, and they didn't send him to prison. She's been trying to get me away from him, and this time she – well, took things into her own hands.'

'Tried to beat the Establishment. She told you all this?'

'Yes, when I faced her with it. She said he was a bad influence, I'd never pass my exams if I hung round with him, all my education would be wasted. That sort of thing.'

Jean sat back in her chair. 'And what do you think about it? Was she right?'

'No! Of course she wasn't. Phil's the sweetest boy. He got misled, that's all, and he's not happy at home. He'll be perfectly all right once he gets a job to suit him, and he says I'm the one person that can keep him steady. We understand each other so well . . . oh, I can't explain, Inspector.'

Jean was thinking very quickly, trying to work out the right thing to say at what might be a crucial moment. She remembered vividly the glacial stare of the china-blue eyes, the totally uncaring comments of Philip Ormrod on his various petty crimes. 'Did you know,' she said carefully, 'that you're not the only girl to think she understands him?'

Theresa looked blank.

'I could show you the record. About a year ago. A girl from Barton Mill Estate. She'd be older than you, about eighteen. Her baby was proved by blood tests to be Philip's – in fact the likeness was strong, just the same hair and eyes. Not the same disposition, I hope, for the child's sake. That boy's a wrecker, Theresa – your mother's quite right about him. If you carry on associating with him you'll be throwing yourself away, not just your education, everything you are. And he won't care – he'll just move on to the next willing girl. He's a born villain, and he doesn't have a heart.'

There was the faintest shade of doubt on Theresa's face now, and the brightness of her defence of Philip had faded. Jean followed up the advantage.

'Have you told your priest about all this?'

The blush returned. 'Well. Haven't been to Confession recently – with all the trouble at home.'

'When you do go, will you tell him everything that's happened between you and Philip – or everything Philip wants to happen? You needn't answer that. I don't suppose he'd be very pleased that Philip isn't a Catholic – or that your mother, who's a good one, went against her Church by meddling with the supernatural.'

Theresa wasn't listening. 'He'd have told me,' she said. 'About any other girl. He hasn't got any other girls, round our way.'

'Possibly not – but he spreads himself around, does your Phil. Theresa, I'm telling you, if you go on as you are doing, you'll be the one that's left with the baby, and he'll be behind bars, for a long time. You can trust me. I'm telling you what I'd tell my own daughter.'

There was a long silence. Jean wondered whether to ask George Parrish to get them tea, then decided against it. Better to let the blow she had struck take its effect. She half-rose. 'All right. Thank you for coming to tell me, Theresa. If your father calls he'll be told the matter's closed. Run along to school now – tell them you've made a quick recovery. Goodbye.'

Theresa managed a wavering smile. 'Goodbye, Inspector.'

Jean sat gazing at the space where the girl had been, young and loving, mixed-up and clever and foolish: and now, please Heaven, doubting. There was no way of knowing whether what had been said would persuade her to give up her young Lucifer. One could talk and talk and do no good, ninety-nine times out of a hundred; but perhaps the hundredth time might be lucky.

Mrs Poley was washing her mother's Coalport china teaset, piece by piece, lovingly, in warm suds. She had never been able to make the imaginary poltergeist smash any of it, but she'd have made even that sacrifice, if it would have done any good, to save the daughter who might even now be standing outside the gates of the mental hospital where Philip worked. Next time she would think of something else, something cleverer.

8 The Cuckoo's Nest

A bedroom door slammed, and Deirdre Street ran downstairs crying noisily. Her husband followed her, catching up with her in the small sitting-room.

'Deiry! What's all the row about? Shut up, somebody'll hear you.'

'Let them. A lot I care! She was listening again, listening, got her ear against our bedroom wall in case we was in there together. She's always at it, I can't stand no more. I was feeding Lyn, and I heard something go bump in there, and I knew.'

Luke drew her down on the comfortable instalment-plan settee, and stroked her hair as she continued to give out the sounds of anger that had become almost mechanical with her. There seemed nothing more he could do or say. Since their marriage, over eight months ago, they had been living with his parents in the two-bedroomed council house that seemed to grow smaller every day, as tempers in it grew shorter. The three of them, counting baby Lyn, in one bedroom, Mr and Mrs Street in the other; the two women sharing the little kitchen, George Street coming home every day from work at Doe Electrics to find the same things – baby-clothes airing round the radiator in the front room, four of them for six o'clock tea round the table that had once comfortably held just him and his wife, Lyn crying as often as not, his daughter-in-law in the sulks and his son the picture of misery.

It had all started when Luke and Deirdre had to get married, because of the baby, just after Luke's job went. The shop he worked in was swept away to make way for a supermarket, and he had no particular skills. The council housing list was enormous; the newly-weds were tacked on to the end of it, with very little hope of a place in years. So they moved in with his parents. Deirdre's family lived in Manchester in a flat: no chance of them helping out. It wouldn't be for long, everybody said at first. But already it seemed like years.

The importance of being a grandmother had appealed at first to Mrs Street, and as a tiny baby Lyn resembled Luke, she thought. Unfortunately she had strong views on the upbringing of children – views which were evidently unpopular with Deirdre, whose only knowledge on the subject had been gleaned at ante-natal classes, not very thoroughly. There were disputes over Lyn's feeds, bathing, clothing and general care. When Deirdre bought her a dummy it was discovered and thrown away with contemptuous remarks. When Mrs Street insisted on Lyn's playthings and effects being kept out of the sitting-room, Deirdre sneaked some of them back, and a battle ensued. Or rather another skirmish in the continuous battle fought between the two women, with the men maintaining an uneasy and fragile truce. George Street thought his son had been well and truly 'caught' by a girl who wasn't even attractive, thin as a rail with short hair still showing faint streaks of the red and green tints it had acquired at the height of the punk craze. He joined his wife in disapproval of the transistor she carried about with her, permanently tuned to a pop station, and the boots she wore from morning till night.

And Deirdre bitterly resented the lack of privacy. Now that she and Luke had got round to love-making again it was unbearably frustrating to know that only a thin wall divided them from listening ears. And this morning was the last straw.

'She thought we was both there, snatching a quick one, I shouldn't wonder, so she listened, the old cow. And that's it, far as I'm concerned, I'm off.'

'Now, now, now,' said Luke, as he had so often said before, and with as little effect, for half an hour later all they owned was roughly packed into two suitcases, Lyn was in her pram with all her toys and clothes piled on top of her, and Mrs

Street was standing at the front door, watching grimly as her unhappy son followed his wife to the gate. He turned.

'Don't worry, mum. We'll be all right.'

'I'm not worried,' she snapped, before taking refuge in her now strangely quiet kitchen, for a cup of tea and a good cry.

A cruising taxi took them to the Town Hall. In the offices of the Housing Department an impassive young woman listened to Deirdre's vehement story and Luke's faint interruptions, then went away for a long time, before returning to say that their names were still almost at the bottom of the list and there was no hope of accommodation for at least two years.

'But we've got nowhere to live!' Deirdre cried.

'Sorry, can't help.' The young woman turned to the next in the queue.

They spent the night in a lodging house near the railway station, having been turned away from three others because of the baby. It was noisy, drunks in the room below and a bathroom next door, constantly in use.

Next morning it rained, hard and steadily. 'I'll go down the Social Services,' Luke said. 'They'll do something, you'll see.'

Deirdre snorted. 'Likely they won't even believe you've got a wife and child if I don't come with you.'

'Oh, they will. They can check I draw the money for you, can't they?'

Neither Tom Darblay nor Jenny Randall was available at the Social Services offices. He was in court and she away with 'flu. The girl who interviewed Luke was very new and very nervous. He left her feeling that she hadn't the least idea what they'd been talking about. 'But if you've already got somewhere to live, I can't see . . .' she said, over and over. Reluctantly she agreed to get on to the Housing about it, sounding as if the prospect terrified her.

After another night in lodgings, during which their door was repeatedly battered on by people driven frantic by Lyn's crying, Luke returned to Social Services, Deirdre and Lyn with him. Somehow he felt it was not a good idea.

This time Tom was there. He listened sympathetically to

the story he'd heard so often, and the usual elements were present – hysterical young woman, ineffectual young man, baby. He telephoned the Housing Department, his deputy's conversation with them having resulted in one of the most confused reports he'd ever read.

At last he put down the telephone. 'Well, I'm afraid it isn't very satisfactory. It seems they did explain to you quite clearly that there's no chance of moving you up the list. The council building programme is suffering from cut-backs, as you know, and on top of that the tenants of Ansty House are having to be moved out because flaws have developed in the fabric. So they'll all have to be rehoused, and that puts things even further back.'

'That's not our fault,' Deirdre said.

'No, it's nobody's fault. But there it is. And they say that in leaving the accommodation you had you've made yourselves voluntarily homeless – in which case they can do nothing for you.'

'Voluntarily homeless?' Deirdre shrieked. 'Do they think we're daft, or something? Call that a home, that grotty little place with no room to turn round and Luke's mum rabbiting on at me all the time?'

'No, of course it wasn't like your own . . .'

'Too bloody right it wasn't. I'd like to see some of them snotty council types putting up with it. And what about *you*? Got a house yourself, have you? Oh, yes, I can just see it, nice little semi up Hilltop with three beds and two recep. A fat lot your sort know about us. Bloody hypocrites . . .'

'Deiry,' pleaded Luke, 'don't. Isn't there some way they could put us in a hotel, till we can get somewhere, like?'

'I'm afraid,' said Tom, 'it's not very likely in your case. You see . . .'

Deirdre got up, Lyn in her arms. 'Okay, I'm off.'

'Where?' Luke was alarmed.

'Down the Town Hall. I'm going to go in and tell 'em what I think, and then I'm going to park Lyn right outside in her pram and walk off. Then maybe they'll take some notice.'

'You can't do that, Deiry!'

'Can't I? You watch.'

'Mrs Street,' Tom said, 'I do beg you not to do anything so drastic. It won't do the slightest good, and you'd be putting your baby at risk. Why don't you go back to Mr Street's parents and talk the whole thing over reasonably? A good talk might sort it all out. Come on, now.'

'All right,' said Luke.

'Not likely,' said Deirdre. 'Here, why don't we squat somewhere?'

'Squat? That's a rather dangerous thing to do, Mrs Street. It would put you on the wrong side of the law.'

'Couldn't throw us out, though, could they?'

'Not by using force, no.' Luke's face was a study in alarm. Tom, sorry for him, yoked to this virago, said, 'The position is that anyone taking up residence in unoccupied property can't be charged with breaking and entering unless they do just that – entering through a door doesn't mean the same thing.'

'So there's nothing to stop us?' Deirdre asked.

'Well . . . If the property were unoccupied and derelict, or semi-derelict, you'd probably be allowed to stay in it provided the owner or landlord didn't require it immediately – and of course if it was clear that you weren't doing any damage to it. There's a row of houses due for demolition in Boot Street, for instance, where . . .'

Deirdre, still clutching the grizzling Lyn, jerked her head at her husband. 'Come on.'

Alarmed, Tom said, 'I didn't mean to suggest you should go there. In fact it would be a very bad idea – those places are full of damp and very unhealthy. They'd be quite unsuitable for a baby. Why don't you go back to the place where you've been staying, and I'll have a think and talk to some of my colleagues about you. We might just be able to fix you up in a hostel . . .'

But they were out of earshot.

Boot Street would easily have won first prize in a competition for the nastiest street in Hartley. The empty houses were about a hundred yards from a soap factory, one of the few factories still going. Some of the houses had already been pulled down, the area where they had been a wasteland of bricks and general rubble, the fencing round it plastered with ancient posters and large, rude chalked messages. From the doors of the houses that still stood, knockers and door-knobs had been ripped.

'I'm not stopping in one of them,' Deirdre said. 'I'm not even going in. Come on.'

They walked and walked, Luke now burdened with their luggage. He wished he'd been firmer with Deirdre, or his mother, or both. He wished he hadn't been daft enough to get Deirdre into trouble so that they had to get married. He was beginning to wish, guiltily, that he'd never seen Deirdre.

They had left the centre of the town and were in what was known as the posh end. Not a lot in the way of derelict houses to be expected here. He pointed this out to Deirdre.

'You never know. And it's nicer walking.' They were on the Moorhill Estate, a development of private houses, all small, detached, Swiss-styled with a lot of wood and large picture windows, dream homes to engaged couples and young marrieds; each with an integral garage and a manageable strip of garden.

Deirdre stopped suddenly. 'Look.'

'What?' Luke, panting, put down the suitcases.

'That.' She pointed to the end house in a row of eight, on the corner of another road.

'What about it?'

'Empty.'

'It's not, there's curtains at the windows.'

'Yes, but don't you see they're all drawn? Means the people are away.'

'Perhaps there's been a death in the family.'

Deirdre shot him a withering look.

'People don't do that these days.'

'My grannie used to.'

Deirdre was surveying the house with a calculating look in her eye. Suddenly she left him and set off through the tiny, open-plan front garden and disappeared round the back of the house, disregarding Luke's cry of protest. In a moment she reappeared, grinning broadly and beckoning him. Reluctantly he joined her.

'Well? You shouldn't be poking round people's houses, you know.'

'Never mind that. Look!' She turned the knob of the blue-painted back door. The door opened. 'Some daft bugger's forgotten to lock it. Come on, we're going in.'

Luke was aghast. 'But we can't! Deiry, it's burgling!'

'No, it's squatting. Nobody's seen us. Get Lyn, quick, and bring the pram inside.'

Cold with horror, he obeyed her.

Brilliant hot sunshine beamed down on the shining expanse of the Majorcan beach. Pamela Anscombe stretched herself luxuriously on the beach-towel and handed her husband Gerald the sun-tan oil.

'Start on my shoulders. Oh, lovely! I adore having my back rubbed. I'll do yours after, promise.'

Dutifully Gerald unfastened her bikini top and massaged the smooth pale-skinned shoulders, whistling softly as though grooming a horse. It was one of those rare moments, he felt, when a man could feel truly glad to be alive, glad to be a young executive just promoted, with a smashing job and a new house, on holiday with a new, very pretty wife, under the bluest of blue skies, the Mediterranean winking gently a few yards away, and, up the beach, a man selling drinks.

Pamela shared his mood. 'Mmm,' she murmured. 'Lucky us. Doesn't it feel to you like absolute years ago that we were at Ringway, waiting for the plane?'

'Centuries. And more centuries since we left Hartley. Filthy old Hartley. Imagine, it's ticking away just as usual. Probably raining there. I can just picture the office – girls clattering away in the typing pool, old Pearson nursing a hangover, customers trickling into the betting shop across the road . . . Fancy a cold beer, darling? I rather think I do. What's the Spanish for it?'

'*Cerveza*. You'd better concentrate on the "Food and Drink" bit of the phrase-book, and forget that stuff about "I want to see the monastery of Miraflores" and "Can you get me a trained nurse?"'

'Oh, I don't know. I wouldn't mind a nice trained nurse, for a change . . .'

Pamela turned and made a face at him. 'You're not having one. Tell you what *I* like the thought of – no meals to cook. Everything ready and waiting, three times a day, lots of gorgeous sea-food and gazpacho and paella, and no boring saucepans . . . Saucepans!' Suddenly she rolled over and sat up.

'Gerry! The cooker!'

'What?'

'*I think I left the gas under the frying-pan.* I'm almost sure I did. We ate breakfast in such a rush, and then the taxi came early – I can't remember taking it off. Oh, Gerry, what shall we do?'

Gerald surveyed her with amused exasperation. Pamela, he had once told her unoriginally, had a mind like a butterfly, darting from flower to flower. The odds were that she'd turned the gas off automatically. Just another Pamela-style false alarm. But she refused to be reassured.

'If it burns through the bottom of the pan it could start a fire.' Her face was pale with fright. 'The house could burn down. We could get back to find no house there. Oh. I'm going to phone somebody.'

'Who, for instance?'

'Mummy's got a key, but it would take her an hour to get there. Joan, of course! I gave her the spare one.'

'Quite sure?'

'Yes, I *am* sure – I'm not a complete fool. Oh, Gerry, I am, though – what a thing to do, leaving the gas on!'

Their next-door neighbour was in, and assured them that their house was not on fire – she was looking at it through the window – but she would go round at once and check. 'Don't hang on, it'll cost you a fortune.'

Comforted, restored to holiday mood, the Anscombes returned to the beach.

But, outside the house on Moorhill Estate, Joan Cliffe struggled vainly with the key. It turned, but nothing happened – the door remained closed. When she shook it she felt the resistance of bolts. Had they bolted it on the inside and left by the back door? It seemed unlikely, but she went round to see.

The back door, too, was shut and unyielding, the windows all with curtains drawn so that she couldn't see in. She began to feel alarmed. It came to her that Gerry and Pam had certainly left by the front door – she'd seen them from an upstairs window, and waved as they got into the taxi. She hurried back into the house, determined to telephone them back and put their minds at rest, all the same.

Their holiday address was not to be found. Whatever piece of paper she'd scribbled it on was mislaid, or thrown away. In a panic she telephoned the police.

Sergeant Parrish took the call. 'Yes,' he said. 'Doors bolted on the inside, curtains drawn. Sounds like something we ought to look into. Thank you for drawing our attention to it.' He radioed the patrol car in which Jean and P.C. Moss were on routine patrol. 'Hartley to Juliet Bravo. Suspicious circumstances at 98 Oakwood Drive, Moorhill Estate. Neighbour who is keyholder reports owners on holiday and house impossible to enter at either front or back.'

The Ford Escort drew up outside number 98. Jean said, 'Anyone who draws all curtains before leaving for their holiday is a fool. Let's contact the neighbour.'

Joan Cliffe was relieved to see them. 'I've felt terribly nervous since I went round there, in case anyone was inside.'

'It's possible someone is. Do Mr and Mrs Anscombe always draw the curtains when they go away?'

'This is the first time they've been away. They only moved in in March. I expect Pam was afraid the sunlight might fade her new carpets and curtains. She's rather proud of them.'

'It's not a good idea to draw curtains – a dead give-away. And it would have been wise of them to let us know they were going – we keep a check on void houses if asked.'

'Very vulnerable,' observed Moss sagely. 'Private estate, end house of a row, only trees opposite.'

'Exactly. You didn't happen to notice any lights on in the house last night, Mrs Cliffe?'

'Lights? Well, no. I don't remember looking out, but I think I'd have noticed . . .'

Jean said, 'I think we'll go and take a look. You'd better stay here, Mrs Cliffe, and we'll come back to you. Oh, and may I have the key?'

The key went in smoothly, turned, and the door stayed closed. 'I thought she might have been one of those women who can't manage keys,' Jean said. 'So much for that.' She peered through the letter-box. 'No sign of life. Let's try the back.'

She had no more success with the back door. The dust-bin was part full, and Moss produced the information that collections were made on a Thursday, so that any rubbish left by the owners would still be there.

Jean stood back on the little lawn and looked up at the house. And, with her sixth sense knew that she herself was being looked at.

'There's someone inside,' she told Moss. His face lit up; recently his duties had been very boring.

'Think it's a siege, Ma'am?'

'I don't see any shot-guns, so far. But you never know your luck . . . Do exactly what I do, will you.' She flattened herself against the wall, her ear close to the wood of the back door, motioning Moss to take the other side. They waited, silently, senses alert.

And in the house a baby began to cry.

'Right! Round to the front. Now, bang the knocker as hard as you can, and don't stop till someone answers.'

The trick worked. Only a completely deaf person could have stood out against Moss's steady hammering. From neighbouring houses people came out to look; and after some four minutes of it the corner of a bedroom curtain was lifted and a face peered round – the sharp face of Deirdre.

'Open the window, please!' Jean shouted. Hesitantly the casement window inched open, and Deirdre asked through the crack, 'What d'you want?'

'I want to know who you are and what you're doing in this house.'

The face vanished. Presently it reappeared and said, 'Why shouldn't we be here? Empty, innit?'

'No, it's occupied, but the owners are on holiday. Come down here and talk. I won't arrest you.'

'Squatters,' Jean said to Moss. Bolts were drawn and the door opened on the chain. Deirdre looked out. Her face was bare of make-up except for her eyes, the lids heavily shaded in purplish-pink, thick black mascara spiking her lashes and a black line drawn underneath them. Moss was reminded of a Hammer film version of *The Fall of the House of Usher*.

Jean said, 'I'm Inspector Darblay, in charge of Hartley Section. Do you know you're committing a serious offence in occupying these premises?'

'No choice. Homeless, aren't we.'

'We'll come to that. Did you break in?'

The bearded face of Luke appeared behind her. 'No, we didn't. The back door was open. And the man at the Social Services told us it was all right.'

The man at . . . Jean refused to face the possible implications of that. She said, 'I don't know what you were told, but the fact remains that you're in unlawful possession of the premises, and I advise you to leave at once.'

Deirdre looked cunning. 'Going to throw us out?'

'No, we can't do that. A County Court eviction order will be made against you by the owners.'

'They're not here, are they. And don't you go thinking you can get in here when we're out, 'cause we're not going, not the same time, anyway. My husband went down the town yesterday and got a load of food in, preserved milk for baby, everything, so we're okay, thank you very much. If them council people won't give us a place of our own we're entitled to take somebody else's.'

'I'm afraid you're not. Can I have your names, please?'

'Find out,' suggested Deirdre, and slammed the door.

'You were great, Deiry,' Luke said. 'Talking to her like that. I don't like it, though, them coming here. How d'you suppose they found out?'

'How do I know? Doesn't matter, anyway. They can't do a thing to us – you heard what that cow said. Come on, might as well draw the curtains now. My God, it's bloody wonderful not being at your mum's.'

Gerald Anscombe's firm supplied his holiday address, and a telegram was sent asking him to call Hartley Police.

'I don't believe it,' he said to Pamela, putting down the receiver. 'I – just – don't – believe it. Squatters living in our house. The police can't get them out because they didn't break in, they walked in.'

'*Walked in*?' Pamela's cheeks went white under their tan, then scarlet.

'Yes, my love. Evidently you didn't leave the gas on under the frying-pan, but you did leave the back door unlocked.'

'Oh, Gerry!'

'Darling, don't cry. Maybe it was me.' But he knew it wasn't. 'What matters is that they got in, and they're still there. The lady Inspector says we ought to go back and serve an eviction order on them. That will make them officially homeless, and the council can put them in a hostel.'

'I don't care *where* they put them. Our home, Gerry, our lovely little home!'

'It'll still be there.'

It was; with rows of nappies on a line stretched across the back garden. They stood looking at it, unable by law to repossess it. For as long as it took the County Court order to come through they would be living in an hotel, with a plentiful supply of bikinis, swim-trunks, towelling robes and semitropic clothes, and very little else. 'I shall disinfect that house,' Pamela said vehemently, 'from top to bottom. I'll send everything to the laundry and the cleaner's. I'll get a firm in to scrub it out. I don't want *anything* of them left, anything at all.'

'What exactly did you say to the Streets?' Jean asked Tom.

'I don't remember the exact words. Something to the effect that if they chose to enter unoccupied property they'd probably be allowed to stay there until the owner demanded possession. I think I mentioned those derelict houses in Boot Street, just as a temporary measure – of course they'd be utterly unsuitable for the baby. It never occurred to me they'd do what they did.'

'Has there been an inquest?'

'Yes.' His tone told her what it had been like. He was increasingly unhappy in his work, she knew, and this last disaster hadn't helped. If only he'd thought before he gave the Streets that daft advice. If only Pamela Anscombe hadn't been scatterbrained enough to leave the back door unlocked. If only people would take sensible precautions before going on holiday, like leaving curtains undrawn and informing the police. If only her job and Tom's didn't conflict quite so often, and always would while he worked for Social Services.

But something told her there were changes in the air, for both of them.

9 A Traveller Returns

Jean was excited. There was little time in her life for the cultivation of friendships. Close as she was to Tom, she sometimes missed the society of other women, the chance to be her own very feminine self, as a change from being Inspector Darblay. Today was a red-letter day: Annie Howlett, her best friend since kindergarten days, was coming home after a four-year absence in Canada.

They had been separated to a certain extent by Annie's marriage to Roger. It had been a disaster of a union – a strong, positive woman teamed with a weak, inadequate man. Annie had struggled on as long as it was at least bearable, then given up. The divorce took a year of more harassment, after which Annie, worn down by traumas, went to Canada. And Jean missed her.

The signals went green; Jean felt that thrill which goes with the arrival of a train bearing someone important in one's life. Then the nose of the London train appeared round the curve of the platform, snaking towards the people surging forward to meet it. As it drew up she looked eagerly for Annie. Annie was the sort of person who'd be in the right part of the train with her luggage organised.

And there she was, looking reassuringly like her old self. Jean had had a ridiculous fear that Canada might somehow have changed her in four years, but she was just the same, slim, vital-looking, handsome rather than pretty, dressed with casual effectiveness (she'd always had rather more style than Jean), swinging along the platform as though her two suitcases weighed nothing. Jean ran forward.

'Annie!'

'Oh, Jean . . .' They embraced warmly, then took stock of

each other. Annie, too, was relieved that time and absence hadn't changed her friend.

'You look terrific!' Jean said.

'*You* look terrific – I look old.' Jean's bright eyes and lit-up face suddenly made her feel journey-stressed. 'I feel old just now, too. Three hours plus from Euston, and what looked like a football crowd mobbing the buffet. I'm absolutely parched for a cup of coffee, and I've got that old-steam-train grimy feeling.'

'Right. We'll go home, get you refreshed and spruced-up, then I'll drive you to your interview.'

'Super. Sure you've got the time?'

'All the time there is. A day off, for you.'

Jean picked up one of the suitcases and they set off for the exit. Outside the station Annie paused, looking round, and inhaled deeply.

'Hartley!' she said. 'It's just the same. Same old view, same old cabs, same old atmosphere.'

'Atmosphere's right – you couldn't really call it air, and the poor old moors must look a bit mere after the Rockies.'

'I don't want the Rockies – they can keep the Rockies. Jean, you know I did swear I'd never come back. But it's great to be home, really great.'

'Good. I've missed you, Annie, I really have.'

Annie exclaimed over the new house; new to her. 'It's far nicer than the old one, and absolutely *you*.'

'Yes, I knew it was, the first time we saw it. We've got it about right now, after a struggle. Come on upstairs. There's the bathroom, and this is your room. Tom wanted it as a dark-room for his photography, but I shot that one down. I'll be making the coffee while you freshen up.'

Annie looked appreciatively round the kitchen. 'It's lovely.'

'Tom's pride and joy. He designed the lay-out and fixed all the units himself.'

'It's all so – homely, this house. So unlike where I was living. Jean, I used to sit in that tiny little room in a huge block of service apartments in Vancouver and play an old record of *Sumer is icumen in*, which you sang best in our kindergarten, remember?'

'No, did I?'

'Yes. And I'd listen to it, and sit and think I've got no family in the world but one friend, and she's seven thousand miles away, so what the hell am I doing here?'

Jean poured coffee. 'What the hell, as you say. But if you hated it, why stay four years?'

'It was . . . survivable. And the money was good, I could save plenty. The job was good, too. And other things. I teamed up with a sweet bloke called Bill – but, like me, he'd come out of a terrible marriage and a vile divorce. He wasn't going to rush into another. Anyway. I finally made up my mind to come back.'

'Why the six months in London?' Jean asked.

'Well, I knew with the job situation what it is up here, I'd better find some temp. work down there first, while I lined up a job here. And it worked – I'm in line for P.A. to the managing director at Crossley Electrics.'

'Great – only about six miles from here.'

'I know. But fingers crossed – I've got to get through the interview, please God. Quiet confidence, poise, that sort of thing, when I'm really shaking inside. This coffee's good. But that's enough of me – how are you and Tom?'

'It's good – a good marriage, Annie.'

'You're a lucky woman.'

Jean laughed. 'What are you talking about? He's a very lucky feller!'

'So when's he back?'

'A couple of days – he's on one of his Social Services courses. And that's the bit that's not so good. He wanted to do the work so much, and I encouraged him. But it's not turned out the way he expected. In a way he's ideal for the job, made for it. He's made of a great fount of concern, sympathy and understanding for people – which is why I love him – mixed in with a real component of damn stubbornness. So he gets too involved, too much across the policy line of the department. It's like a Samaritan getting a call for help and rushing round to the address so that they can cry on his shoulder. He gets hurt, and he's beginning to feel frustrated and inadequate.'

'I can imagine.' Annie had always liked Tom, and envied Jean just a little the possession of him.

'It's hard for me to say to him, look, love, take three weeks' holiday, it's owed to you, and let's have a break – go somewhere that's a complete change of air, where you can sit down and really work out whether you can go on with the Social Services.'

'Why can't you say it?'

'It would be forcing his hand – pushing him into making a decision. I don't want to do that. But I feel there's going to be a break, and it won't be long before it happens, without my interfering. This course he's gone on may turn the scale – I don't know . . .'

Annie was stirring her second cup of coffee, round and round, thinking. She said, 'Jean, I wonder if you could do me a great favour. It's about Roger. I have to meet him. I have to talk to him.'

'Why?' Jean thought of Roger as the kind of man no one would seek an interview with if it could be avoided. She hoped very much that her friend wasn't having second thoughts about him. Annie's next words reassured her.

'I can't have a repeat of those months before the divorce. It was so utterly awful – midnight phone calls, the whining, the crying, the threats of suicide, all the misery-guts of it – I just can't.'

Jean remembered it well. 'Does he know you're here?'

'I wrote to him. I'd like to see him before the interview, talk to him and spell it out – get it from him straight that he'll never bother me again. That way I'll be easier in my mind when I face the firing-squad at Crossley's.'

Jean looked doubtful. 'You think that's the way to handle it?'

'Yes, I'm sure. If I move back to Hartley, sooner or later he's going to find out, and if he starts pestering again it'll make it impossible for me to stay. I *have* to have it out with him – but I need someone there. I do need some support. I really would appreciate it if you were around.'

'Of course I will be.'

'Thanks.' They smiled at each other. It seemed

marvellous to Jean to have a friend to talk to again. 'What time's your interview?' she asked.

'Two-fifteen. I'd like to fix this meeting with Roger around one, if possible.'

'You ring him and sort out a time, and I'll fit in with it.'

They agreed that the meeting was not to be an alcoholic one – that was one of Roger's main troubles. Tea, and not too much sympathy. Annie was going to see him in the sitting-room, while Jean waited in the kitchen in case of a summons.

At ten minutes to one the bell rang. 'Well, here we go,' Annie said, looking fraught. Some good ideas never seem as good when the actual moment comes.

She led him into the kitchen. He looked even less impressive than when Jean had last seen him. Some men look young at forty-five – Roger looked forty-five. He was beginning to stoop, and his face was set in down-drooping lines. Jean wondered why the bright Annie had ever looked at him.

He greeted her wanly and offered a limp hand.

'Hello, Roger,' she said. There was no temptation to add, 'Nice to see you.' 'I'll bring some tea shortly.'

Annie and he sat facing each other across Jean's hearth-rug.

'How are you?' Roger asked, as though expecting an ominous reply.

'Just fine,' she said briskly. 'All right, Roger, I'll tell you why I wanted to meet.' His woebegone doglike gaze irritated her.

'You look terrific, Annie,' he said.

'Thank you, we'll take that as read. Look, Roger: I'm back. At least I think I'm back, to settle down in Hartley.'

'What d'you mean, you think you're back? I didn't under-stand from your letter.'

'Well – it's up to you. Whether I settle here or not.'

'I don't understand.'

'Then I'll spell it out. From the moment our marriage broke up – for the year it took to get the divorce – well, you remember what happened.'

He sighed. 'What in particular?'

'I remember all too well, even if you don't. I was in Mary's flat. You'd get drunk, all hours of the day or night. You'd phone up, crying down the phone, saying you were sorry.'

He turned his head away, staring at the empty grate. 'Don't go into that . . .'

She went on relentlessly. 'Turning up at my work, drunk. Writing letters to me, phoning my friends, and crying.' She hoped he wasn't going to start now, but he was still, mercifully, sober.

'It's all over,' he said.

'Well, that's what I want to know. It has to be over.'

'All right, it is.'

She fixed him with a resolute eye. 'I'm coming back to Hartley, Roger. We're divorced. You have to tell me that *that* behaviour will never happen again. If you think there's even an outside chance that it would, I won't come back. I'll keep well away from here, from you, for the rest of my life.'

'That was four years ago, Annie. I'll not bother you.'

'You absolutely promise?'

'Yes. I'm over it. And you.'

She wanted very much to believe him, though there was still doubt in her mind. 'Thanks.'

He said, 'I don't drink as much as I used to. I realised I was ruining my health.'

'That's good news.'

He got up. 'Is that it, then?'

'You've absolutely promised?'

'Yes.'

'Then that's it. Let's have a cup of tea with Jean. Then I have to go off for this job interview.'

'I don't want a cup of tea. If that's it, I'll be on my way.' There was a dangerously emotional look in his eyes, and a tremble in his voice. 'Will we . . . will we keep in touch at all? Will you ever want to meet me again?'

'It's not a good idea.' She was trying to sound firm, but not unkind.

He gulped, and turned away. 'Say goodbye to Jean for me.'

112

'Of course.' She followed him into the hall.

'Goodbye.'

'Goodbye, Annie.' She shut the door behind him.

When Annie returned to the house, later in the afternoon, she was radiant. 'I got the job!' she called out from the hall.

Jean emerged. 'Wonderful! Terrific!'

'Looks like a good job and good pay. But it was close – five other girls interviewed.'

'And *you* got it. Marvellous, Annie.'

'Tonight,' Annie announced, 'we're going to go out on this town and let it know I'm back. And it's on me – you pick the restaurant.'

Jean patted her waist. 'Something modest, Annie, in the way of eats. It's all right for some, but I've got to fit into the uniform. And when I don't, it shows.'

'Well, you choose. Now – I've got to change into jeans, pop into town for an hour and buy some good, sensible managing director's P.A. tweeds – God help us. Tweeds, me!'

'Where will you find those?'

'Oh, Burnley, I'm sure. There's bound to be a little shop in Burnley selling sensible tweeds – yuk.'

'There isn't another vacancy – for a managing director's secretary?'

'Why? You're not thinking of . . .'

'I've heard rumours down the grape-vine. There's a new boss moving in on us, any time now, and the story goes that he doesn't like women in office. Or anywhere much, I gather. A holy terror, it's said. I may be getting windy about nothing, but I've got a sort of nasty feeling . . .'

'Never mind,' Annie said, 'hope for t' best and get ready for t' worst.' It was a remark Jean was to remember.

The Wethergate Hotel and Restaurant had started out as a pub, simple and unadorned. Progress had brought to it gold flock wallpaper, a lot of banked-up potted plants, fibre-glass beams, paintings by local artists for sale, and not at all a bad menu. Space being limited, a trellised partition, entwined with more plants of the climbing variety, separated the restaurant area from the lounge bar.

Annie looked round her. 'This is all changed. Good thing we put our finery on.'

'Better or worse, do you think?' Jean enquired.

'I don't quite know – I'll have to get used to it, then I'll tell you.'

'When were you last here?'

'Not since I was courting.' She shuddered slightly.

A waiter was hovering with menus.

'Thank you,' Annie said. 'We'll have a bottle of wine to start us off. Red, Jean?'

'Prefer white, please.'

'Then half a carafe of the house red, and the same of white.'

The waiter bowed and vanished.

'Funny,' Jean said, 'he was English. They're like hens' teeth in restaurants round here. So, what are your plans for tomorrow?'

'I've got to start house-hunting.'

'What a prospect . . . You'll hunt in our area, I hope?'

'Of course I will,' Annie said. 'I'd not forgotten, you know – your family made three house-moves from the time you and I were around eight till we were fifteen – and each time our new homes were further apart.'

'I remember. I hope we never, never have to move house again – it put years on us. You know the price of houses here, I hope? I mean, you're not going to have a heart attack when you hear some of them?'

Annie laughed. 'I'll try to bear up. I made some money in Canada – enough to put a healthy deposit down, thank goodness, so that's a start.'

The waiter was again hovering. 'Are you ready to order, ladies? I can particularly recommend the chicken suprème and there's a very nice duck and orange.'

They studied the menus. 'Right,' Annie said, 'Duck and Outspan for me.'

The waiter looked slightly puzzled. 'Duck and orange, madam?'

'That's right. And fish soup to start.'

Jean chose Dover sole and avocado with prawns. The

wine arrived, Annie poured for them both and took out a cigarette.

'You don't mind?' she asked. Then, 'Oh, my God. Look. Roger.'

He was there, unmistakably, sitting on a stool in the lounge bar, ordering.

'Do you want to leave?' Jean asked. 'We can cancel the order and go somewhere else.'

Annie shook her head. 'It's stupid of me – of course, this was always one of his pubs. I ought to have remembered – after all, we used to come here. No, it would be childish to leave. Why should we be driven out by him? We'll stay.'

'If you're sure . . . he's seen us.'

Roger was looking at them, expressionless. Annie nodded, as though to a distant acquaintance, and he nodded back, then looked away.

Jean raised her glass. 'Well – here's to the evening!'

And after all they were allowed to enjoy their meal. They talked and talked through it. 'Do you remember?' they asked each other, again and again: schooldays, O-Levels sat together, boyfriends, partings and meetings, the infatuation one of Jean's brothers had had with Annie . . . They laughed, drank their wine, and Jean felt more relaxed than she had done for a long time, for Tom's company was more stressful than it had been once, and with Annie there were no stresses. She looked forward so much to Annie staying in Hartley – to having a friend again.

If Roger would let her stay. Jean had been watching him, still at the bar throughout their meal, drinking steadily. She drew Annie's attention to him. 'He's had a lot. I'm afraid I've been counting. Nine large ones. Come on, we'll go, we can pick up the bill outside.'

Annie hesitated. 'Jean, in a way I don't want to run away. In a way I'd like to see this out. I'm going to live here – I'm bound to be bumping into him from time to time. I have to know whether he's going to be a problem.'

'I'm afraid he is, quite soon. I think he's crying.' Roger was leaning forward over the bar, his shoulders heaving.

'Oh, God, he is. Are you in the phone book? Yes, of course you are. We've got to leave. The test will be how much more he's going to drink, and whether he phones me, weeping, at your house. He knows I'm staying with you, after all. Come on.'

They walked out, carefully not looking at Roger, but aware that he seemed not to notice their going.

Back at the house Annie said, 'Mind if I stay up? I shan't sleep if I go to bed, waiting for him to ring.'

'I'll stay up with you. What about a brandy, as we didn't have time for a liqueur at the Wethergate?'

'Suits me.'

Jean fetched the bottle and they settled down, Jean as nervous as Annie, for she had a stake in her friend's staying in Hartley. 'How long do you think we'll have to stay up?'

'If he hasn't made a drunken call by two o'clock, he won't call. And then maybe I can consider him cured.'

'I'll drink to that.'

In a telephone kiosk in Hartley's shopping precinct Roger was also drinking. His nine Scotches had made him staggering drunk, but he was refreshing himself from the bottle of vodka he'd bought at the bar. After two long swigs from it he put it back in his pocket, laid a row of coins out along the shelf of the kiosk and studied them owlishly, swaying. Then, with difficulty, he found the right page of the filthy, coverless telephone directory. Dar, Darabi, Darbar . . . the letters were swimming before his barely focusing eyes. Darblay, T. That was it. He poised a coin in the slot: it fell off and rolled on the floor. With a curse he poised another, then took another swig from the bottle.

There was a perfunctory tap on the door before it opened. Young P.C. Farley, temporarily posted to Hartley as a replacement for Roland Bentley, was regarding him reproachfully.

'Good evening, sir. Making a call?'

'What's it to you?' Roger growled.

'You don't *seem* to be making a call, sir. And from your breath you seem to have been drinking.'

'What you going to do, breathalyse me for driving a telephone?' Roger grinned foolishly. The constable seemed unamused.

'I'll be back this way in an hour, sir. I just don't want you to think you can sleep the night in this box.'

'I . . . I've got a bloody home to go to.'

'Then why don't you do that, sir – go home?'

Roger tried to think of an explanation. He came up with, 'I'm waiting for a bloody telephone call.'

Farley raised his eyebrows. 'At one-thirty in the morning, sir? I'll be back this way in an hour. I trust you'll be gone by then.'

He left. Roger stared morosely after him, lurched, almost fell, and returned to studying the laid-out coins.

The wall-clock in Jean's kitchen pointed to the hour of two. Both women looked up at it.

'He hasn't phoned,' Annie said. I think I'm going to be all right.'

'Great. Thank God for that. We could have taken the phone off the hook, but it was better to do it this way.'

'Yes.' Annie yawned hugely. 'Thanks for staying the course with me, Jean.'

Jean, too, yawned. 'That's all right. Pleasure. Goodnight, Annie. See you in the morning.'

She was conscious of a great relief as she climbed the stairs. A battle had been won: she would keep her friend after all.

10 The New Broom . . .

'Well, this is it,' Tom said. 'The end of the line.'

'Are you quite sure?' Jean had sensed what was coming from the moment he'd got home. Preoccupied, not taking in what she said, lingering over the pre-supper drink so long that she put the casserole back in the oven. Then it came out, the story of the last milestone on the road to Tom's resignation: an impossible situation, his defence of a colleague in trouble, his temper lost.

'I'm completely sure. I was never going to make it as a social worker, was I? I started off starry-eyed, thinking I was the solution to the human condition. The first time I stepped over the mark and got carpeted, I thought, fair enough, just a beginner.'

'The Murphy affair.'

'That's right. Then I began to find out that there were more hazards than straight stretches. If you bend over to get a case investigated, you're interfering unduly; if you play careful you're guilty of neglect. Can't Win, department of.'

'Sounds like my job,' Jean said drily.

'Much more than that. The law's the law, something cut and dried, but there aren't any rules in our game. A child dies of parental ill-treatment, so we didn't call often enough or listen to the neighbours. Child's taken into care, the parents immediately turn into some sort of angels and everybody hates the brutal S.S. I'm sick of it, Jean, sick of it. Today was the end. I've resigned, and I'm not going back on it.'

Jean sipped her drink, not tasting it. 'So what next?'

He shrugged. 'Find a job. Write round. Watch the ads. Pull any strings there are to be pulled. Somebody somewhere must want a good design draughtsman, even if I've got to travel to and from wherever it is. I don't mind if I've got to be away five days a week and home only for weekends. Would *you* mind?'

She shook her head. 'I don't mind anything that's going to help.'

'But there's one thing. If I stay out of work for long I'll be living off you, and I don't want that – not a second time. That's what's kept me from resigning before.'

She put her hand over his. 'It needn't have done. It didn't part us, last time, and it won't this. I'll go along with anything, Tom.'

His look thanked her without words.

'Now,' she said, 'if you don't want supper ruined we'll eat it. And we'll have a bottle of wine to celebrate.'

'Celebrate what?'

'Your freedom. A new start. Beginnings.'

Annie telephoned. 'I've found it!'

'The house?'

'Absolutely the right one. Perfect.' Her voice vibrated with eagerness now that the shadow of Roger had lifted. 'On the edge of Elfield, just about where the village begins. It's not much more than a cottage, grey stone, looks as if it grew out of the landscape, and I absolutely love it, Jean.'

'Great. Is it handy for Crossley's?'

'Right side of town. Anyway, I'm going to buy a car – I can afford to, out of what the house isn't costing. When can you come and see it? It's empty and the key's next door, so we could go any time.'

Jean thought. 'What about Monday morning? I've got it free. We'll go about ten, if that's all right, then I'll have time for shopping afterwards. Yes, it'll have to be Monday.'

The cottage was everything Annie had said. Foursquare, separated by a strip of garden from its neighbour, it looked on to green fields and moorland back and front. Its stones were tinged with lichen, its slate roof showed here and there touches of green, where birds had dropped seeds. Inside, a long room that had been the kitchen ended in a deep fireplace with a beam above it. The staircase was concealed by a small door.

'It's like a doll's house, a perfect doll's house,' Annie said. 'I've always wanted a staircase like that. And this room – imagine what it'll be like when I've got at it!' They wandered round, paused to admire, discussed the décor, furniture, curtains and rugs, organised the neglected garden into a blend of flowers and vegetables. Annie's taste was more developed than Jean's, but they agreed well enough.

'It's just what I dreamed of in that poky place in Vancouver. I did mean to move to somewhere near you, but there wasn't anything on the agent's books, and then I saw a picture of this, and I knew it was for me.'

'We'll make contact,' Jean said. 'I'll be out here for a bit of peace and quiet so often that you'll get sick of me.' Looking out at the calm landscape, she sighed. 'Peace and quiet! I doubt if there'll be much of that around tomorrow at the Nick. He arrives in the morning.'

'The dreaded new boss?'

'Sub-Divisional Superintendent Hallam. Keep your fingers crossed for me.'

If Jean had only known, Hallam was at that moment surveying his future kingdom from the car park. Big, ponderous, looking and behaving older than his forty-eight years, he was very different from the mild, amiable Superintendent Lake. And he was looking forward to his new appointment, very much.

For eight years, stuck in a groove, he had been a uniformed Chief Inspector in a small divison, fretting and fuming under what he considered to be the rank incompetence of his superior. Up to that time his progress upwards had been good. Then came the halt which had turned him into the police equivalent of Albert Edward, Prince of Wales, waiting for Queen Victoria's throne. With the promotion to Hartley he felt that the throne and the crown were his at last.

There was little in Hallam's life but work. He wouldn't have called himself a workoholic – that would have been too frivolous a word, suggestive of one of the vices he looked on with disfavour, having been brought up as a Methodist by parents with strict principles. Even now he sometimes appeared in his local chapel as lay preacher. He was unmarried. He managed his own housekeeping to his satisfaction, being essentially meticulous and efficient in small things; he had had little to do with women, didn't care for them, on the whole. WPCs in his previous division had no reason to remember him with pleasure.

George Parrish and young Farley were on duty. They looked surprised, and snapped to attention as he entered and greeted them, taking in them and their surroundings in one long, raking glance.

'I'm Superintendent Hallam,' he announced unnecessarily.

'Sergeant Parrish, Constable Farley. Welcome to Hartley, sir.'

Hallam asked, 'The Inspector? Inspector Darblay?'

Parrish coughed apologetically. 'I'm afraid we must have got our wires crossed, sir. We weren't expecting you till tomorrow – the Inspector's off today.'

Hallam smiled, a cold tight smile which he imagined to be warm and irresistible. 'No wires crossed, Sergeant. I was going to come tomorrow. Changed my mind. Sometimes it's more educational to see what a place looks like before it's cleaned up for the new Superintendent's visit, yes?'

Parrish looked wary. 'Yes, sir.'

'Yes, sir what?'

'Er . . . nothing, sir.' Parrish was conscious of being on trial, almost the subject of cross-examination.

'Do I know you, Sergeant?'

'No, sir, I don't think we've met before.' I'd have bloody well remembered if we had, Parrish thought.

'Are you busy at the moment, Sergeant?'

'Nothing urgent, sir.'

'Ah. Then perhaps you'd like to give me a guided tour of the station, followed by a guided tour of the section?'

Parrish was sure he would like no such thing. He tried to parry the order veiled as a request. 'There's very few in the station – no one in CID, sir.'

Hallam beamed. 'That's fine. I just want to put my head round some doors.'

Resigned, Parrish put on his jacket, dimly aware that he was being criticised for having taken it off. Hallam turned to

121

Farley, who had been making himself as inconspicuous as possible.

'And how long have you been in the Force, son?'

'Five years, sir.'

'Married?'

'Yes, sir.'

'Settled in the job? Enjoying it? No complaints?'

'None, sir.'

'Good lad.'

Parrish volunteered, 'Constable Farley's with us on temporary attachment, sir. Now, if you're ready – I'll show you first the parade room, the interview room . . .' He led Hallam from one place to another, conscious that sharp eyes were on everything and mental notes were being taken. 'Putting his head round doors' meant that Hallam could observe everything out of place which would have been straightened or tidied away if he had arrived the day after. Jean's office was orderly, as she had left it, but Parrish sensed Hallam's disapproval of her unseen presence there. Gloomily he wondered whether this man would ever take part in a friendly knock at the billiard table in the recreation room, as Superintendent Lake had sometimes done. It seemed improbable. His mind went back to the short but dreadful reign of Inspector Robins, the martinet with feet of clay, who had forbidden such things as smoking within the public view and making private telephone calls from the desk. Certainly, Hallam's manner was civil enough, which Robins' hadn't been. But George Parrish's mind misgave him.

The tour of the section was made in Hallam's car. They took the town area first, all points of importance, the railway station, football stadium, hospital, Town Hall, notorious traffic junctions, streets with a bad reputation. Hallam said little about it, only remarking that he had travelled through Hartley a good many times, particularly when a mate of his, Dave Brewster, had been stationed there.

'And of course Joe Beck, I know him – he was a sergeant in Colstone in my time. Ten years back. I was pleased to hear he was on the strength at Hartley. A good man.'

'Yes, sir.'

They had climbed out of the town, up on to the hills to the east of it, looking down at Hartley huddled in the valley, a conglomeration of shades of grey and black, a few mill chimneys, long disused: Cleckworth Mill, Pharaoh's Mill, among them. They got out of the car.

'You can more or less see the boundaries of the section over there, sir. East Hartley. And then over to those chimneys just behind the quarries – that's Norton-le-Willows.'

'Aye.' Hallam scrambled to a higher point through a gap in a low stone wall, and breathed deeply. 'What ozone. Hundreds of years of dark satanic mills, and still man never ruined the purity of the air of the moors. Nothing like it . . . When I see people smoking in air like this, I think they must be off their heads. You don't smoke, do you, Sergeant?'

'Yes, sir.'

'Pity. I used to myself, of course. Quite heavily. I gave it up the day I got this promotion, never been tempted to go back since. That's self-discipline for you. Worth it, to get back clean lungs and a clean palate . . .'

Parrish had an intuition that the section was going to receive some lectures on self-discipline. He wondered what, if any, the Superintendent's hobbies were, and received ananswer without putting the question.

'Go in for birds at all, do you, Sergeant?' Parrish did a quick double-take and decided he must mean pigeons, not the non-feathered kind.

'No, sir. Haven't really got the facilities for keeping them. We're pretty crowded.'

'Family man, are you?'

'Yes, sir. Four children. Eldest son in the Force in Burnley.'

'Good, good. Pigeons, now, I'm quite a fancier. Soon as I get settled into the new place I'm going to build a loft. Care to give me a hand?'

'I don't know that I'd be much good at it, sir.'

'Well, never mind. What's your name, Sergeant?'

'Parrish, sir.' (As if he hadn't caught it the first time, Parrish thought.)

123

'That's your surname.' (Implication, let's be pals.)

'George, sir.'

'And are we going to get on well, George?' There was no doubt about this in Hallam's mind, it was merely a rhetorical question. He saw himself as a man's man, able to be one of the lads while maintaining inflexibly his superiority over them. So Parrish would be 'George' henceforward, but *he* would never be 'Albert'.

'I hope so, sir,' was the not over-enthusiastic reply.

'It's got to be more than hope in our game, George. Necessity, isn't it, for the new Superintendent to find allies, men he can trust? To ably assist him through the changes he's going to make. I'll need some allies, George. I mean, it's quite something, isn't it? A woman running a section . . .'

Before Parrish could agree or disagree with this Hallam had turned away and was once more scanning the valley. He mused. Parrish was to find out that he had quite a line in musing, with appropriate quotation.

'D'you know that line from Carlyle, about the time, when, quote, "The Ribble and the Ayre rolled down as unyet polluted by dyer's chemistry"?'

Parrish shook his head. He didn't know any lines from Carlyle.

'That's gone. Worse, now. Dark, collapsing, bankrupt satanic mills. The English just got fed up working, didn't they? Now, I put that down totally to moral decay – bankruptcy of the spirit.' (He had used that line with great effect from several platforms.) 'However, there are a few of us left who didn't get fed up with the idea of hard work, and I'm one of them. As you and your colleagues are about to find out.'

Parrish didn't doubt it. This was just the sort of way Inspector Robins had gone on, and it struck an ominous note.

Hallam did some more musing with intent. 'I've never yet found anything perfect in the way the Force organises itself. There's always room for improvements – sometimes little ones, sometimes major ones.'

Parrish knew what was coming.

'The Inspector,' Hallam said. 'A woman. Bit of a turn-up for the books, isn't it – a woman in charge of a Section?'

'We thought so, sir, when we first got the news. But she's turned out to be a terrific boss.'

It was not the answer Hallam had been expecting or hoping for. He said, 'Really?' in the flattest of tones. Parrish met his eyes steadily.

'Yes, sir.'

'Hm. I find that hard to believe. However, we'll see. The important thing is, she may be your boss, Sergeant, but I'm *her* boss. I do have feelings about women doing jobs they weren't meant to do.'

Parrish said nothing.

'I think I have to talk today to Mrs Darblay. Could you give her a phone when we get back?'

'She's off today.'

'She may be, but if she's about I think she'd better come in.' His gaze was directed to the other side of the valley, as though he knew that two tiny dots of colour in the Elfield area were Jean and Annie, still in the front garden of the empty cottage, and could discern them with magic telescopic eyes.

A strangely depressed Parrish accompanied him back to Hartley. Normally an optimistic character, he felt the wind of change on the back of his neck. He wondered how Joe Beck would react. It had taken Joe so long to adjust to serving under a woman Inspector, and now . . .

As though the elements were in tune with his mood, it started to rain.

11 ... Sweeping Clean

Jean and Annie drove back to Hartley in quite the opposite frame of mind. On the way they giggled, and sang snatches of songs they had sung together at school. 'Do you remember *The Rambling Sailor*, and how the words used to corpse us? I never thought old Miss Wattie knew what they meant. And that awful thing, the Cats' Cantata we called it?' They rendered snatches of the Cats' Cantata, to the surprise of passing motorists: two respectable-looking young women, apparently yelling their heads off.

'Let's go to the delicatessen, and pick up some stuff for lunch, then all I'll have to do is put Tom's supper in the oven,' Jean said.

They collected vol au vents, cheesecake, and a confection of celery and nuts. Healthily hungry, Jean laid the table. The telephone rang.

'Sergeant Parrish, Ma'am.'

'Yes, George?'

'I've been trying to get hold of you, Ma'am. The new Superintendent's arrived.' Parrish's tone was flat.

'But – he's not due till tomorrow.'

'Yes, Ma'am.' There was a suspicion of a sigh. 'He said as much himself.'

'Oh. All right, George, tell Superintendent Hallam I'll be along after lunch. I've got a friend with me.'

'Well, he's in your office now, Ma'am, and he says he'd like to see you if possible.'

Very irritated, Jean said, 'Tell him I'll be half an hour.'

'Yes, Ma'am.'

'Trouble?' Annie asked.

'I hope not. But he's arrived a day early and he wants to

see me. Damn. Let's have a quick bite, and I'll go and get it over.'

Parrish was at the desk when she arrived. She knew his expressions well, and this one was not his sunniest.

'Mr Hallam's still in your office, Ma'am,' he said.

'Is he. Where's Sergeant Beck?'

'He's at Stretley School, giving a Road Safety talk.'

'I see. Can you organise some teas?'

'Yes, Ma'am.'

Superintendent Hallam was not only in her office, but sitting behind her desk, reading her files. She repressed her instant feeling of resentment, and smiled.

'Good morning, sir. Inspector Darblay. Welcome to Hartley.'

'Thank you, Mrs Darblay.' His own smile was mechanical. *Mrs* Darblay? Was this form of address going to continue?

He closed the file he was reading, got up and strolled to the window. She recognised the old ploy for making an interviewee feel initially uncomfortable. But she was not an interviewee, and it was her office. She moved to the vacant chair behind the desk. Hallam turned.

'Yes, all the appearance of a nice little town you've got here, Mrs Darblay.'

'Yes, sir.'

He seemed to be working things over in his mind, ticking them off as he said them. The next one was, 'You took a Monday morning off?'

'Two weeks notice I gave, sir. As usual.'

'Ye-es, I checked that. Monday mornings, of course, are not the best times to take off. Mondays are for sorting out the problems and reports of our busiest nights, Fridays and Saturdays. Yes?'

Jean opened her mouth to say that she had her oldest and best friend staying with her, after an absence of years, but instinct told her that he wouldn't be impressed. 'Yes, sir,' she said. Suddenly she wished very much that he had not caught her in plain clothes. Uniform would have lent her the feeling of authority which she knew he was trying to undermine.

Point Three was about to be made. 'I've just been taking a glance through Section CID reports, and I'm afraid, Mrs Darblay, I have to raise a criticism. A number of significant cases for a town of this size seem to have been hanging fire for a heck of a long time.'

'That's possible, sir.'

'*Obvious* – Mrs Darblay.' He watched her face for the frown of irritation at the way he intentionally addressed her. How would he like it , she wondered, if the Chief Super were to call him Mr Hallam instead of giving him his title.

He went on, 'I've had a lot of experience of non-metropolitan areas like this – worked long years in towns like Hartley. I can tell you a thing or two about them. Because they don't need the intensity of policing that an immigrant area, say, in Birmingham needs, there's a tendency for people to sit back in these hamlets and admire the scenery. And *sometimes* fall asleep on the job.'

'I haven't noticed that in this Section, sir.' It wasn't time yet for her to show direct opposition. It is a truism in the Force that anyone under the rank of Superintendent is just a copper who takes orders, and that once a copper becomes Superintendent he becomes a policy maker, a man of power.

He waved towards the files. 'I would have said from these CID reports it was obvious you haven't noticed it. Why are your CID not getting results, why are your men not on their toes?'

'I think they are, sir.'

'These reports say they aren't.' She refused to react, waiting for the next stroke. It was more forceful than she had guessed. 'I'm going to be absolutely blunt with you – Mrs Darblay. I believe that the main task of an Inspector in charge of a Section comes down in the end to man manage-ment. I'll be more blunt, and say I find it extraordinary that a woman should be doing this job. In words of one syllable, I don't think you should be here, running Hartley Section.'

They looked at each other, cat and dog, male chauvinist and woman in authority, and she read 'enemy' in his small blue eyes. She was shocked, a cold feeling around her heart. What she mustn't do was to show it. She said levelly, 'I don't think that I wish to comment on that, sir.'

He leaned back, complacent, looking forward to Point Four. 'No, you don't have to. I think there are a lot of good jobs in the Force for a woman, and I think you should be in Headquarters building or somewhere, employed in one of them. D'you know a quotation I'm rather fond of, Mrs Darblay? Quote, "Seek to be good, but aim not to be great, A women's noblest station is retreat." '

She was nettled to rising point by now. 'No, I don't. I suppose another favourite quote of yours is "Be good, sweet maid, and let who will be clever"?'

'As a matter of fact yes, it is,' he said, unblinking.

'I disagree, sir – that I should be employed elsewhere.'

'I'm sure you do. You've been nine months in this job and I'm sure that if you made a request that you wanted to move on, it would be sympathetically considered.'

Her stare was mutinous. 'I'm not moving anywhere, and I'm staggered by your suggestion.'

Hallam shrugged. 'As I said, I'm your new boss. I want the best policing for this Section. It's clear that things need tightening up around here. That requires leadership — *strong* leadership. I'm not going to disappear, Mrs Darblay, in case you're hoping I shall. I think you should start to give some thoughts to your future in the Force. Meanwhile, of course, you shall have my co-operation.' He collected his hat, coat and stick. 'I'll be present at parades tomorrow,' he said, and left.

Jean sat very still, her eyes on the shut door. She was stunned, upset, coldly angry. Soon she would talk to the men, but not for a few minutes.

In the car park Hallam encountered Beck, and greeted him warmly.

'I remember you, Joe. And I've heard about you down the years.'

'I hope it was good, sir.'

'All good, Joe.' Beck wondered what the effect would have been on this man if the news of his Irish adventure had spread. Determinedly matey, Hallam asked, 'D'you still have that old Brough Superior motorcycle you used to drive?'

'No, sir, it's now down to rheumatism and a Raleigh upright.'

Hallam nodded. 'Before you go in there, I want to ask your advice on an urgent matter. What's t' best pub in Hartley?' It was his Decent Chap question, the Man's Man, the boss who gets on terrifically with the lads, and Beck recognised it for exactly that. He said without expression, 'Crown and Sceptre, Bridge Street, down the hill, first on left, sir.'

'Thanks. I'll be at parades, tomorrow.'

'Welcome to Hartley, sir.' Beck went into the Nick, to be greeted by Parrish with the news that Ma'am wanted to see them both.

'Eh? I thought we were getting a rest from her today. And I thought Mr Hallam was due tomorrow.'

Parrish replied, 'Well, he's an early bird. And he's been looking for worms.'

'Has he, now?'

Jean was still sitting at her desk. They noticed that she looked taut and strained. She gestured them to sit down.

'Well. Have you both met our new Sub-Divisional Superintendent?'

They said they had, and Beck added, 'I served under him in Colstone near ten years back.'

'And what was that like?'

Beck thought. 'A good man. A bit of a plodder – but fair. A bit religious – Methodist. Professional bachelor. A bloke who's always got his nose to the grindstone whether there's work to do or not.'

Jean said, and they had never heard the note in her voice before, 'I walked in here and he informed me in no uncertain manner that he'd decided, on somewhat dubious grounds, there's evidence of slackness in the policing of this Section. And more to the point – he said he didn't want a woman in my job and I should start to think about my future in the Force.'

Parrish showed dismay, Beck surprise; but not a lot of surprise.

'He's not allowed to say that to you, Ma'am,' Parrish said. 'He may be our new boss but you were appointed here and I

130

don't think he's any right to question your appointment. If you take my advice, Ma'am – if that's what he said – I think you should send a memo to someone at Headquarters about it. What do you say, Joe?'

'I wouldn't send a memo critical of a man who hasn't really started yet in the job, to Headquarters.'

'You're right, Joe,' Jean said.

'I'm sorry to hear this, Ma'am. It's not been my experience that the new Super. was like this before.'

Parrish added, 'We will support you, Ma'am, to our best endeavours.'

She had relaxed a little. 'Thank you, Joe, George. I just thought you'd better know straight away that we've got off to a good start.'

Outside her office Beck said, 'Looks like we've got a problem.'

'With a capital P,' Parrish observed. They were quiet as she came out, passed them with a preoccupied nod, and went to her car. 'Some day off,' he added.

Beck had taken over the desk and Parrish was still around when they had a visitor.

'Good afternoon, Sergeants. Police Constable Prentice reporting for duty.'

P.C. Prentice, Roland Bentley's replacement, was very young. He was shorter than Bentley, thickset, large-eared, bubbling over with enthusiasm. If he seemed, and was, a shade raw, underneath that there was a confident public entertainer waiting to be let out. His smile was wide and all-embracing. Beck gave a theatrical groan.

'Oh my God, another new arrival. I don't think I can take the pace.'

Parrish beckoned Prentice round the desk. 'Come round here. We were expecting you.'

'Not like some,' Beck muttered.

Prentice hovered. 'I've left my motorcycle in the kerb round the side. Is that all right?'

Beck threw out a theatrical aside. 'Good, he's a motor-cyclist. He won't be with us long.'

Parrish gave him a reproachful look, and formally introduced them both to Prentice, who looked puzzled. 'I'm to report to Inspector Darblay.'

'Yes, well, you'll have to wait on that, the Inspector's not here.'

Beck put in, 'But look pretty sharp, lad, the Superintendent is.'

'Oh. Maybe I could just brush my hair, and things?'

Beck started back in feigned surprise. 'Hair? His hair looks lovely, doesn't it, Sergeant Parrish?'

'Mm. A little black to be in fashion around here, lad – we go for the greying worried look.'

Beck, catching on, asked Prentice to repeat his name. At least they'd have a bit of fun, even if the Super. was looming over them.

'Prentice. David Prentice. My friends call me Davey.'

'Well, we'll call you Constable Prentice until we get to know you,' said Beck heavily. 'Then God knows what we'll call you.'

Parrish kept up the ribbing. 'Prentice, do you know how to make tea?'

'Certainly I know how to make tea, Sarge!'

'A piece of advice, lad, for the long years you may not be with us. Quality tea-making comes first here, Law and Order a poor second.'

The new recruit looked from one to the other of them. He was not quite on their wavelength yet, but he had things up his sleeve. 'You sound like a couple of jokers, Sergeants. Have you heard the one about the Irishman and the cup of tea?'

Beck exploded. 'Oh my God, he's not an Irish joke-teller? Harold, or whatever you call yourself . . .'

'Davey.'

' . . . I think I'd better take you to the parade room for coiffure, introduce you to the tea-making arrangements, and then we'd both better lecture you on the tradition of not telling Irish jokes in this station. Come on, lad.'

Parrish watched them go, amused. He was less amused to see Hallam re-enter. This time there was no atmosphere of bonhomie about him.

'Mrs Darblay still here?'

'The Inspector went home, sir.' They were both perfectly aware of Hallam's use of the prefix, and Parrish's implicit correction of it. Parrish was conscious that he was being marked down for non-cooperation. Collaboration with the enemy, more like.

'Get her back,' Hallam ordered. 'I want to see her again. Urgently.' He disappeared into Jean's office.

Jean and Annie were drinking tea when the call came. 'Hell's teeth,' Jean said. 'I can't believe it.' She had only had time to give Annie a short breakdown of the situation. It had been a relief to get home, away from the blight Hallam had cast, and now she was to be wrenched back into it. She drained her cup. 'Perhaps I'll be allowed to have a snack in my own home one of these days.'

'I'm sorry,' Annie said. 'Worrying for you.'

'I'll live. You'll be all right? Got the spare key in case you want to go out? Right, see you later.'

Parrish was gloomily writing up notes. He paused to tell Jean that the other new posting, Constable Prentice, had arrived.

'It's all happening today, isn't it,' she said.

'Yes, Ma'am. But not necessarily for the best.'

'You can say that again.' She went into her office, where Hallam was again sitting at her desk, going through files. He nodded her into the opposite chair, and, silently fuming, she took it.

'Something I meant to take up with you earlier,' he said, hardly looking at her, as though she were someone come to mend the telephone. 'I got a call two days ago from an old friend of mine, Superintendent Shipley, you know, over at Cannock.'

'I don't know him, sir. I've heard of him.'

'He's retiring, Mrs Darblay.'

'I know that, sir.'

'Do you also know that he lived here in Hartley some years back?'

'No, sir, I didn't.'

'And the publican of the Sportsman's Arms is a very good friend of his.'

'Yes, sir?' This was going to be a prolonged fencing match.

'So,' Hallam put his hands together, steeple-wise, 'when he decided to have a retirement party, the publican friend offered his pub. And the publican friend put in for an extension of permitted hours until one a.m. for this party.'

'Yes, I know this, sir.' And he knew she knew.

'Next, Mr Shipley and the publican are staggered to find that you intend to go before the magistrates and object to this extension.'

'Yes, sir.'

'Well, I've spoken to Mr Shipley and told him that I'd discuss this with you and persuade you to drop the objection.' He waited for her to climb down, to placate him.

'I'm afraid that's out of the question, sir.'

'And how is it out of the question?'

'I've been instructed by the Chief Superintendent to object.'

Hallam drew a deep breath. He had expected to be able to walk this one, and he was not pleased. He looked at Jean, disliking her personality, her femininity, her attitude to him, her existence on earth. He had magnanimously handed her the chance of bowing her forehead to the ground before him, and she was not taking it. 'I get the impression, Mrs Darblay,' he said heavily, 'that you're suggesting I don't know a damn thing about Force procedures. Correct me if I'm wrong. You have a pub in your Section – the Sportsman's Arms. You decide, as occasionally happens, that you don't like the pub or the publican, an application for an extension of permitted hours is made, you give a nod to the chief Superintendent and he instructs you to object.'

'That's not the case, sir . . .'

'I haven't finished. This is a retirement party for a man who has had an entirely distinguished career of over thirty years serving the Constabulary. Among the people who will be at this party will be many senior officers past and present. *You* can get on this phone and say to the Chief Superintendent that because of these unique circumstances you really have been thinking about this, and that this must be *one* occasion when an exception should be made. And I want you to get on this phone and do just that, Mrs Darblay.'

What seemed like a half-hour pause followed. There was a squeal of brakes out in the street. In the desk area somebody laughed, then stopped short as though remembering that strange ears were listening. Jean's eyes were very bright, the set of her mouth resolute.

'I'm sorry, sir,' she said. 'I can't now do that.'

Hallam's voice rose with his temper. 'Are you deliberately misunderstanding me, Mrs Darblay? I know Chief Superintendent Gates and I know he has a high opinion of you, and if you do get on the phone and tell him you've changed your mind, my bet is that he'll change *his* mind.'

Jean said coolly, 'I'm sorry for Superintendent Shipley. We've objected to extensions of permitted hours at the Sportsman's Arms before. Residents have made complaints about noise and disorderly behaviour around the pub within the last three months. I have to go through with this. It would look like nepotism to make an exception in favour of a police function.'

Hallam let another silence fall. He was forming phrases in his mind, rolling them over, angry with her for her insubordination, glad that she had given him the chance to hit out at her. He let her wait for his verdict.

'This is about the smallest favour that I could have asked you, Mrs Darblay. I now have to go back to Jack Shipley and tell him that I, the new Superintendent, was unable to persuade an Inspector under my command to make this phone call.'

He rose and took his coat from the stand. Jean felt she was living through a dream which kept repeating itself. At the door he looked back at her.

'I won't forget this in a hurry,' he said.

12 The Turn of the Screw

Because one new arrival promised to be not much of a laugh, Beck and Parrish felt they were entitled to have some fun out of another. As Prentice deposited two cups of tea on the desk, Beck solemnly introduced him to another young and newish constable, Harry Newton.

'This is our new man, Harry. Arthur Prentice.'

'*Davey* Prentice.' The correction was made very mildly. They shook hands.

'Arthur is patrolling Two Area,' Beck told Newton. 'Could you take him down there on your way to Three Area?'

'Yes, Sarge. I've just got to get my mac.'

Parrish was drinking tea. 'This is the second good cup you've made us, Prentice. We may have to revise our earlier confidential opinion that you have no future in the Force.'

Beck nodded. 'Excellent. And the biscuits are bloody good, as well. What are they called?'

'Chocolate coconut crunch. My mum always buys them.'

'Give my compliments to your mother, Constable. Tell her how much George and me appreciate a woman of discerning taste.'

'Thanks, Sarge.'

Newton appeared, macintoshed. 'Right, let's go.'

Beck called Prentice back. 'Oh, Arthur . . .'

'*Davey*, Sarge.'

'Of course, Davey. There wasn't mention of this on parade. But there have been a number of burglaries in Two Area recently, and we reckon we've got the villain's description. He's been seen.' He winked, almost imperceptibly, at Parrish.

'He's big,' Parrish said. 'A big chap.'

136

'Six foot six plus,' Beck added.

Prentice looked from one to the other of them, worried. 'Oh.'

'And he carries a hammer,' was Beck's next contribution. It inspired Parrish.

'He's left-handed, so if he hits out at you, expect the blow to come from the left – yes?'

Beck nodded. 'And he always takes a transistor radio with him on the job, tuned to Radio One. If you hear Radio One playing . . .'

Prentice was getting more and more puzzled by the contrast between their serious manner and the grotesque things he was hearing. 'Radio One — and he carries a hammer?'

Parrish maintained a perfectly straight face. 'Yes, and he wears women's clothes.'

'You're having me on, Sarge.'

Parrish turned to Beck. 'Having him on. D'you hear this, Sergeant Beck – are we having him on?'

'We're not having you on, son.'

'And if you see him,' Parrish warned, 'don't tackle him before you call the police. But not us. He's a bit more than we care to handle.'

Newton called, 'Coming, Arthur?'

'*Davey*,' said Prentice mechanically, looking back at the two Sergeants as he went out. Beck called after him.

'Remember, dressed as a woman.'

'A ballet dancer!' added Parrish.

Left alone, they laughed uninhibitedly. 'Took it like a lamb,' Beck said. 'Remember how we sent Roland up when he first came?' They reminisced, finishing the tea and biscuits. Beck, who had been waiting for an opportunity, said with elaborate casualness, 'Speaking of ballet dancers . . . did I show you this?' He produced a wallet, and from it a colour photograph of a young girl of elfin beauty, poised in a dancing attitude. 'My Carol. Taken the other week. Seems to be quite the star of the ballet class. She says they're going to put on the whatsit, Nutcracker, and she's dancing somebody called Clara, who seems to be important.'

'Good for her. Grown, hasn't she. Of course, she'll be ten

now. Not far off our Lucy's age. Pity you can't see her oftener.'

'Aye. But it could be worse.' Much worse, he reflected.

Parrish was having a quiet night on desk duty when a call came through. 'Yes, ma'am?' he said. 'Yes, ma'am. Gayton Road. Telephone number? Yes. We'll be there as soon as possible. Thank you.' He called Prentice, who replied, on his personal radio, that he was checking shops, half-way down Elvira Street.

'Good. Go to the bottom, left, then first right, Gayton Road. Report of sound of a window breaking at the back of shop, Eldon Electronics, 14 Eldon Parade.'

'On my way, Sarge.'

Prentice might be new, but he had sharp eyes. Just outside the open door of Eldon Electronics' stock room he took in a curious scene. The burglar was a small, ratlike man, old enough to have known better than to conduct a burglary as he was trying to do. Or perhaps he was past it. Furiously, incompetently, he was wrenching at an old pram which was stuck half in and half out of the stock room rear door. 'Blast you!' he said aloud, 'come on in, can't you?' His efforts were hampered by the torch he held in one hand. Twice he dropped it, cursing.

At last the pram was through. Prentice waited for him to load it, thereby providing evidence of burglarious intent. In they went – torches, lamps, small electric fires, neon tubes, anything portable, until the pram was so full that objects kept falling off the top, to the thief's increasing fury. Prentice would have liked to see him try to manipulate the lot through the rear door, but action had to be taken. He appeared, majestically, in the doorway.

'Who are you and just what are you doing here?' he demanded.

The little man's reaction was quick. He seized a three-bar electric fire and flung it at the constable, then charged at Prentice, taking him by surprise. The struggle was brief. The younger, fitter man soon gained control and, holding his prize in a half-nelson, spoke into his personal radio. Parrish answered.

'Burglar at the premises, Eldon Electronics. And I've got him. Mobile required.'

'Good lad. We'll get a mobile to you.'

'D'you want a description of the burglar?'

'Not necessary, Prentice.'

Undeterred, Prentice pursued his revenge. 'Well, he's six feet seven inches, carrying a hammer in his left hand, with a transistor in his right tuned to Radio One. He's wearing women's clothes, a very fetching net-over-taffeta two-piece in a kind of rose pink with black sequins and diamanté.'

'Thank you, Prentice.' Parrish's tone was grim.

'I think you'd describe it as a ballet outfit, Sarge,' Prentice said innocently. In his grip the writhing burglar was demanding, 'What the bloody hell's this? What the . . . women's clothes? Ballet outfit.'

'You shut up,' Prentice told him. He had thoroughly enjoyed his evening.

Jean had not enjoyed morning parades, with Superintendent Hallam looking on. She was beginning to dread his ominous silences, the way his brain could almost be heard ticking over as he composed his next speech of criticism. And he was a genius at nit-picking, extracting evidence of inefficiency and slackness from nowhere and somehow making them sound convincing. She knew that he would be delighted if she were to burst into tears; he probably thought women did that all the time, and was faintly puzzled that she hadn't done so yet.

He was nettled, too, that Beck, Parrish and the others hadn't closed ranks to support him. They were men, weren't they, members of the great anti-women union? They'd been alarmed when a woman had first been put in charge over them, so what had gone wrong that they had this attitude to her, admiring and protective? It was beyond Hallam's comprehension, and he was determined to break it down.

The magistrates' court that was to decide the future of ex-Chief Superintendent Shipley's retirement party was assembled, the three magistrates in place on the bench, a scattering of people in the body of the court, among whom was Hallam, an elderly man beside him. Jean, sitting alone, kept her eyes away from them.

The first application to be made was for an extension of the permitted hours at a social club, for a prize-giving ceremony.

'Have the police any objections, Inspector?' asked the clerk.

'No objections, your worships.'

The chairman of the magistrates pronounced that the application was granted for an extension of hours to eleven-thirty p.m. Again the solicitor rose.

'I am obliged, your worships. My second application is for an extension of permitted hours at The Sportsman's Arms, Hartley, on the night of the 25th of this month, the hours to be extended from ten-thirty that night until one a.m. the following morning.

'I appreciate, your worships, that this application is a little unusual; perhaps I might explain. On that evening Mr Shipley is holding a party to celebrate his retirement. As your worships may well be aware, Mr Shipley has recently completed over thirty years as a police officer attaining the not insignificant rank of Chief Superintendent. On the occasion of his retirement he wishes to entertain his many friends and colleagues at a party. Some of his colleagues will be unable to leave their duty until ten p.m., and will then have to travel a distance to reach the function. For this reason, to enable Mr Shipley to say farewell, in a sociable and proper way, to his colleagues, I am instructed to make this application. The usual letter has been submitted to the court, and, if your worships wish, Mr Shipley is available to give evidence in support of the application.'

The magistrates nodded, smiled, conferred briefly, and indicated that they had no need to hear Mr Shipley. Inspector Darblay was called. She stood, a solitary figure with all eyes upon her. There was tension in the air.

'Your worships,' she said, 'I am instructed to resist this application.'

A sort of rustle ran through the court.

'As your worships will recall, I have objected to extensions of permitted hours at these licensed premises on previous occasions. Residents in the vicinity of the Sportsman's Arms have made many complaints to the police during the last

140

three months. The complaints allege excess noise, disorderly behaviour by customers leaving the premises, and inconsiderate parking of cars by patrons. I have received written notice from solicitors representing a number of the residents, that it is their intention, unless the situation improves dramatically, to object to the renewal of the licence at the Sportsman's Arms at the next licensing session. For these reasons I am instructed to object to the application which has been made.'

She sat down. There was a conference among the magistrates, heads together, longer than their last one. Then the chairman announced that they would retire to consider the application.

Jean read through her papers while they were away, unnecessarily. She knew how much hung on the magistrates' decision. If it supported her, more ammunition for Hallam. If the application were granted, he would crow over her and her authority would be that much diminished.

They returned. The court stood, reseated itself, and the solicitor waited. The chairman adjusted his glasses and spoke.

'Mr Elwood, we have given this matter our most careful consideration. We would like to record our appreciation of Mr Shipley's long and conscientious service in the police, and we would like you to convey to him our best wishes for a long and healthy retirement. We have listened to what Inspector Darblay has said about this application. We sympathise with the people who live in the vicinity of the Sportsman's Arms, and with the police officers who have the unenviable job of trying to mediate between the parties involved; we feel that should the problem continue it may only be resolved by a decision of this bench. It is not our intention today to anticipate that decision. However, we feel we must refuse the application for the extension of permitted hours.'

The solicitor bowed. 'As your worships please.'

Outside the court, Hallam was waiting, the grey-haired Shipley with him. He stepped into Jean's path.

'Mrs Darblay. I just wanted to introduce you to my friend, ex-Chief Superintendent Shipley.'

She put on a smile. 'Hello, sir.'

Shipley stared at her outstretched hand, turned on his heel and walked away, followed by Hallam, whose back view seemed to swagger.

She stood for a moment, feeling the shock of the worst public snub she had ever taken. Then she rejoined Beck in the area car. He looked at her enquiringly, seeing the answer to his question in her face.

'Well, we won, if you could call it winning. If we'd lost it would have amounted to just about the same. Joseph, things are going to be a bit different at Hartley from now on.'

'Yes, Ma'am, I think we can all look forward to a future with Mr Hallam that's not one long round of laughs.'

She, Tom and Annie had finished supper, a meal she hadn't relished. She was not in the habit of bringing work home, unless it were something she could usefully discuss with Tom. But this could not be shaken off, and they were sympathetic listeners, trying to help.

'If it weren't such a small thing to have made an issue of,' she said. 'He only had to speak to the Chief Superintendent himself to get it all sorted out. But he had to make a test case of it.'

Tom said, 'Sure it wasn't rigged? Seems funny to me, a top copper picking on a pub with a bad name to hold his wake in.'

'How do I know? It sounds elaborate, but I'm beginning to think I wouldn't put anything past our Mr Hallam. I'm getting paranoiac about him. If he walked into the Nick tomorrow with horns and a tail it wouldn't surprise me.'

'He sounds quite the wrong man to be in authority over anybody,' Annie said. 'How did he come to be appointed?'

'Sheer bad luck – for us. It's not that he's all that great – far from it. He could have got where he is now when he was thirty-six – some do. Instead he got stuck in the works, and it took him twelve more years, getting soured off in the process. It's the worst type – starts off well, goes nowhere with it – eight years sitting at a desk, grafting away and hating the world – then *we* get him, and he takes it out on us. On me.'

142

Tom put his hand on hers, distressed for her. 'You're not going to let him get you down, are you, love – not going to give in?'

'Don't worry. He won't make me resign by twisting my arm. I shall stay put and let him do his worst – which he will. He's dedicated his life to making mine intolerable.'

Superintendent Hallam had cast aside the cares of office for one evening. Equipped with hammer, saw, nails and white-wood, he was beginning his new pigeon-loft, unconsciously humming a hymn, a catchy little thing with a rather stern moral. He was looking forward, very much, to the beginning of another day.

13 The Devil's Tunes

The streets of Hartley were quiet and dark. Particularly quiet and dark was Gas Street, a narrow way that ran behind a row of Victorian shops, and a taller building. There was only one sign of life in Gas Street at two a.m., a figure moving about a door at the back of the large building, to the accompaniment of a whining noise. The noise stopped. The severed lock fell to the ground, the door opened, and the figure melted inside.

A wandering tomcat investigated a van which was parked without lights at the end of Gas Street, decided that it held nothing of interest for him, and stalked off. No watcher at a window, or light sleeper, saw or heard anything suspicious. And no patrolling constable came near.

Constables Davies and Prentice had attended morning parades and were on the first lap of routine patrol in a CID car, Davies driving.

'Not a lot doing today,' Davies remarked. 'Boring, you might call it. We could stop for a coffee when we've done Area Three, if you like.'

'Wouldn't mind. It's a long time to next refs. Don't know about you, Davey, but something about driving around gets me starving . . . It's all right to stop, is it?'

'So long as we've got our radios on.'

As though it had heard him, his radio spoke. 'Hartley to 4218. Reported break-in at Rechabite Hall, Oldham Street. Back door in Gas Street entered, property missing.'

Davies replied. 'On our way, Sergeant.' To Prentice he said, 'That's coffee, that was, Davey.'

The Rechabite Hall was gloomy, outdated, neglected. It

belonged to a property firm which would for preference have had it down and an office block in its place, but that the economic future for new offices in Hartley was poor and the project would have ended in expensive demolition and a permanent hole in the ground. The Independent Order of Rechabites had forsaken it long ago; if they still existed they practised their teetotal principles outside Hartley. The key was held by an old newsagent, Bill Biggs, four doors away. His son now ran the business and he kept himself busy by helping out and doing such odd jobs as letting people into the Hall and taking the money at functions.

The two constables surveyed its shabby front entrance, plastered with announcements of meetings, rallies, charity sales and concerts. The Hall, being cheap, attracted less glossy functions than the Pantheon, a one-time cinema with a bigger seating capacity. On top of older posters was a new one, in yellow and black, announcing the appearance of The Tykes pop group. Prentice, who fancied himself as a disco king in his off-duty moments, said 'Never 'eard of them.'

Old Bill Biggs was waiting for them near the entrance. He was elated because something had happened, at last, on his territory, but nervous in case it could somehow be blamed on him, and his prized responsibility taken away.

'Come in, come in,' he welcomed them. 'You were quick off t' mark. I'd nobbut phoned five minutes sin'. Eh, they're in a right state, these lads, don't know where to put themselves.' He led them through the hall itself, a cheerless place painted yellowish-drab, on top of which somebody had attempted the sort of primitive frescoes to be seen on the walls of mixed communities: garish oils of clowns, boxers, Monroe and Chaplin, spacemen and wild animals. Old texts were above the platform and windows: Wine is a Mocker, Strong Drink is Raging, Look not upon the Wine when it is Red, at the Last it Biteth like a Serpent and Stingeth like an Adder.

Prentice looked round it. 'This place could put you off your ale. Did you hear the one about the Irishman and the missionary?'

'No,' Davies said. Biggs bustled in front of them through a door at the side of the platform into a barely furnished, musty-smelling room where four youths were sitting. Four young, miserable faces were raised, and on one at least there were traces of tears.

A tall, fair-haired boy got up. 'Glad you've come,' he said. He was very thin, as they all were, dressed in the uniform of youth – jeans of various colours, T-shirts with THE TYKES printed across them and shabby leather jackets spangled with badges. Three boys were white, one coffee-cream.

'Well,' said Davies in the approved manner of investigative policemen, 'what's all this?'

'Our gear,' the boy said. 'Instruments. Gone. We put them in here last night, locked up, and this morning they'd gone.' He spoke with a middle-class accent; Davies guessed him, rightly, to be a first-year university student.

'That's right,' Biggs said. 'Back door broke open and t' whole lot cleared out. Done by a professional, if you ask me.'

Davies took names. Denny Adams, lead guitar and synthesiser, Jake Birstall, base guitar and vocals, Whitey Joel, the brown boy, drums, Bram Horrocks, keyboard. Two more, who appeared from the other dressing-room, were named as Dale Chisholm and Bunny Law, respectively roadie and electrician.

'Pretty small fit-up you've got,' Prentice commented.

Denny shrugged. 'All we can afford, mate. I can only work out of term-time, and the others when they fit it in. We saved like hell to get the band together. And now this . . .'

'My mum took a job to pay for my drum-kit,' Whitey said. 'Saved it all up.' He wiped his eyes with his sleeve.

'Well, let's have the damage.' Davies took down from Dale Chisholm the approximate value of the instruments. It horrified him. When he added up the total it came to a staggering sum.

'You'd better come down to the station,' he said, 'and we'll sort it out there. Got a van, have you?'

'Aye, they left us that,' Bunny Law said. 'Kind, wasn't it – didn't even siphon off the petrol.'

Together Davies and Prentice examined the break-in point. It was undoubtedly the door leading from the dressing-room into Gas Street. The old lock had been neatly and professionally drilled round and removed. Davies nodded. 'Doesn't look like kids, though you never know. Kids would have seen the posters and known the stuff would be around. Right, let's go.'

Bill Biggs followed them to the front door. 'Will there be detectives? Like on t' telly, takin' prints, dabs? They can take mine, I don't mind what they do, so long as they get culprit.' He was eager, elated; it was better than making up bundles of newspapers and helping his son to sell pencils and postcards. The Tykes were one of the few pop groups he'd seen in the flesh. He was thrilled to have them there, picturing their glamour-lit lives – girls, drugs, parties, jet travel. Though they didn't look much in that line; quiet sort of lads, he'd have said . . .

Jean, who was interested in everybody, also found them a welcome change from the routine customers of the Nick. While Beck interviewed them she sat listening, looking from one to the other. Denny, the boss of the outfit, level-headed, answering questions sensibly, inwardly bitter. Bram, whose name turned out to be Bramwell, after the Salvation Army chief of staff, and who had started his musical career as a boy cornet-player in a brass band. Whitey, second-generation Yorkshire, who had never had a job and found being with The Tykes next thing to Heaven. Jake, slender and girlish-faced, his hair dyed platinum-silver. Dale the roadie, older and tougher than the others, the one who booted out trouble-makers at gigs and argued up fees with skinflints. Bunny, the only long-haired one, moustached, with a certain resem-blance to a young Charles the Second.

Jean was familiar with the symptons of drugs, from pot to the hard stuff. She saw no sign in any of the boys, which ruled out the possibility that the instruments had been sold to buy supplies.

Beck asked, 'What about insurance?'

'No way,' Bunny said. 'You know what the premiums are? Couldn't be done in our league. They reckon they've got to charge at the top because of the risks involved.'

'Seems they're right, son.' Beck glanced at Jean. So no insurance fraud was involved.

'And you don't know anybody in Hartley – anybody who'd want to spite you?'

Dale answered. 'Not a soul. We only took the booking because somebody else dropped out. Whoever ripped us off did it to flog the stuff, there's a big market for it.'

'Right,' Beck said. 'We'll get someone round all the music shops and second-hand dumps. There's Bangalore Fred – a bit near home, though. There's two or three marts in Coppins Street. Or they could have driven straight off to one of the big towns, and gone from one dealer to another. It's not the brightest prospect, lads, but we'll have a go.'

'Get Constable Newton on to it,' Jean said. 'He'll know where to look.'

'Right away, Ma'am.' Beck went out.

'There isn't much of a chance, miss, is there,' Dale said. It wasn't even a question.

'Not a lot. We'll do our best, but you'll have to be prepared for nothing turning up.'

'Joe Loss's brother,' Bunny said. 'Dead loss.'

Nobody laughed.

'We worked hard to get this outfit together,' Denny said. 'My dad gave us something towards funds, because he believed in us, but apart from him and Whitey's mother that's been it. We'll never get that much together again.'

'So what will you do?'

He shrugged. 'Go home. Sell the van for what it'll fetch.'

Dale said, 'They won't give us any of the takings money now, will they, miss?'

'I shouldn't think so, in the circumstances. It's a pity you're not insured against this sort of thing.' She looked round the young, defeated faces, and was taken with a sudden idea.

'Have you eaten today?'

Denny shook his head. 'They wouldn't feed us that early at the pub. We were going to get some coffee when we had a break.'

'Then I'll tell you what. You can have something here. Fish and chips do you?'

They stared. 'What, here?' Denny asked. 'I didn't know you gave people food . . .'

148

'Well, we're not a restaurant, but it's been known. Yes?'

'Yes, please!' Their faces lit up. For the first time even Whitey smiled, showing beautiful teeth. They had had the worst shock of their young lives: someone had done something rotten to them, and now someone else was being kind – the awesome police, so unpopular with their age-group. It was the one bright spot so far in a day of disaster. They fell on the parcels of fish and chips brought by an intrigued Prentice, who had never been so close before to members of a profession he was still inclined to idolise. He stayed with them while they ate, drinking in their tales of travel and adventure, of the punk riot from which they hadn't expected to get away with their lives, of the country house where they'd played at the coming-of-age party of the son of the family, and been put up in such luxury as they didn't know existed; of girl groupies and their almost unbelievably shameless ways.

They were quite sorry to leave the Nick, and Jean was quite sorry to see them go, visitors who had given no trouble and touching gratitude. Their addresses had been taken – they would be told at once if any of their missing instruments turned up. But neither Jean nor they entertained much hope of that. The last she saw of them was the fair wistful face and silvery hair of Jake at the back window of the van. He had developed the beginnings of a crush on her.

'Well,' she said to Beck, 'you hear a lot of bad things about pop groups, but I reckon there's not a lot wrong with our Fab Four.'

'There will be, if they keep on at that game. Can't help it. Too many temptations.'

'Oh, come now, Joseph. What do you know about it?'

'Only what I've seen at some of these Rock Festivals. Things I wouldn't sully your ears with, Ma'am.' Shaking his head, he began to enter the cost of six helpings of cod and chips in the petty cash book.

No music-shop or second-hand dealer within a twenty-mile radius would admit to having received any of the stolen property. A mention in a regular radio report produced no results. The sad story of The Tykes provided a bit of welcome

149

sensation for Bill Biggs's son's customers, the broken door of the Rechabite Hall was repaired, and the posters on the wall began to peel off in the rain.

More than a fortnight later Parrish got a mid-evening call for assistance. He radioed Prentice. 'Sound of Music department again. Trouble at the Hand and Flower, Market Square. Barman's not making too much sense, but it sounds like a punch-up.'

'Be there in two minutes, Sarge.'

There was a lot of noise going on in the public bar of the Hand and Flower. Inside, Prentice found a violent struggle in progress on the floor. Two men were rolling over and over, clawing and grabbing at each other, and a knot of customers huddled away from them. Behind the bar a small wizened man was looking on in alarm. At Prentice's entrance he lifted the flap and scurried to the constable's side.

'Thank God you're here, lad! He's gone off his rocker, nobody can't do owt with him.'

'Who's he, then?'

'Mr Heaviside. T' landlord.'

Prentice approached the scuffling, shouting pair on the floor.

'Now then,' he said in his loudest voice, 'that'll do. Out of it. Come on, out of it.'

The note of authority got through to them. The bodies disentangled, and Prentice saw that one was a big, purple-cheeked, bald man, the other a slight youth who hardly looked old enough to be in a pub at all. He scrambled to his feet, while his opponent lumbered up slowly, and he was trembling and tearful with rage.

Ever since joining the Force Prentice had yearned to do a comic policeman act, beginning with 'Now, now, what's all this, then?' Before he could get any of it out the youth was bawling at him.

'He broke my tranny! Smashed it up, look.' On the floor by the bar lay a small transistor radio, its aerial snapped off and a great dent in it as though someone had taken a hammer to it. 'Rotten sod. Swining old bastard!'

The big man was gasping with exertion, wiping his

sweating face. 'You shut your mouth,' he told the youth. 'Aye, I did break his blasted machine, officer, and I'd do it again, and him too if he brings another of them things in my bar.'

'Just a minute,' Prentice said. 'Let's have a bit of quiet, shall we? Who started this?'

A girl came forward, small, sharply pretty, dressed disco-style. 'It was him!' She pointed to the landlord. 'He set on Ted for doing nothing at all, bashed him about.'

'That's right,' said Ted. 'Look at my tranny – new, it was, and he's bust it up. I'll want compensation for this, Mr Heaviside.'

'And we've got witnesses!' The girl looked round the customers for support; there seemed to be plenty of it. The safety-pins in her ears swung to and fro – Prentice was relieved to see that they were attached to ear-rings.

'Get out,' Heaviside shouted, 'get out, the lot of you. And that means you, too.' He jerked his head towards Prentice, who said, 'I'm afraid not, sir. If this lad's charging you with assault we'll have to take it further.'

'I *am* charging him!' Ted pointed to a cut on his chin, which was now bleeding. His girl-friend tenderly mopped it with a handkerchief. 'I'll have him up in court, I will – I hope he goes behind bars for it.'

Prentice began to scribble, happily, phrases like G.B.H. common assault, and damage to property. Heaviside knocked the notebook out of his hand and came at him like a bull, but the younger, spryer man jumped aside, nipped behind the bar, where the little barman seemed to be rooted in a state of stupefaction, and radioed for a mobile.

Because Heaviside showed signs of violence in the car, he was taken straight down to one of the cells. Ted Driscoll still seemed shaken. He sat in the interview room, his girl-friend holding tight to his hand, and gratefully accepted tea from Parrish before making his formal statement. He had been sitting at a table with Debbie, drinking a half and eating onion crisps, with the transistor beside him. It had been playing quietly, though he admitted that the volume might have varied a bit. Nothing rough. 'Not Heavy Metal, you know, middle of the road.' Nobody round them minded. Then Heaviside had come round the bar, roaring, pulled him to his feet, bashed him in the face and thrown the transistor across the room. He'd tried to defend himself and been thrown to the ground, which was when the barman must have called the police.

'All right, you can go home,' Parrish told the boy and girl. 'You'll be informed when you're wanted to give evidence.'

'And he will get charged?' Ted asked. He felt his chin tenderly. 'I think there's a tooth come loose with that clout he give me.'

'He'll get charged, all right. Go on home and get your mum to see to your face.'

When they had gone he went down to the cells and looked through the peephole of the one which held Heaviside. What he saw caused him to whistle softly to himself.

'He was *asleep*?' Jean looked up from the notes taken the night before. 'After all that commotion, in the pub and the car?'

'As a baby, Ma'am. I'd to wake him to get his shoes and the usual stuff, then he went off again.'

'Drunk?'

'No smell of it.'

'And this morning, how did he seem?'

'Surly. No thanks for taking his breakfast in. And he wants to go home.'

'He would. All right, I'll take a look at him.'

Heaviside was sitting on the edge of the bed, hands dangling between knees, staring at the ground. He looked up as she entered, and growled 'Who are you?'

'You know perfectly well who I am, Mr Heaviside. We've met often enough when I've made my rounds of inspection.'

'Oh, aye. I thought you were one of them young women cops. Well, seeing it's you, Inspector, I want out of this place, quick. I've got my pub to see to. I can't trust that Arnold to do owt right.'

'I'm afraid it's not quite as simple as that. A charge has been laid against you, which means that you'll have to go before a magistrate. You've had the charge read to you?'

152

'Aye.'

'And you agreed that the events happened, but insisted that you were within your rights in assaulting Mr Driscoll and destroying his transistor, and afterwards attacking Constable Prentice and attempting to prevent him from taking notes?'

'I was, that.' His slightly bulging eyes, faded blue, met hers in a hard stare. Somewhere in her mind a memory stirred, too faintly yet to be recognised and revived. She knew that there was no need for her to question him, with two signed statements leaving no doubt of what had happened, but curiosity and an instinct she trusted drove her on.

'Do you mind telling me,' she asked mildly, 'how you make that out? Justified assault doesn't seem a very good answer to the charge.'

'Everybody knows I won't have it. That's my answer.'

'Won't have what?'

'That hellish row, in my pub.'

'You mean the transistor?'

'Is that what they call it? The Devil's Mouthpiece, that's my name for it.' A dark flush was creeping into his heavy cheeks. Jean took care to speak quietly and unprovocatively.

'You mean you don't like pop music?'

He banged a fist down on the edge of the pallet. 'Filth! Poison! They that feed on corruption shall become as worms. The Evil One sends up his jigs on a fiery blast, and they enter into the ears of the godly to destroy the brains in the head and cause them to boil as a cauldron.' Heaviside's eyes seemed to stand out further, and the veins in his temples were swelling. Jean went to the breakfast tray, the food on it played with and abandoned, poured a cup of tea and offered it to him. 'I think you need this, Mr Heaviside. It's a bit cold, but it won't do you any harm.' She watched him as he sipped it mechanically before asking, 'You don't hold a Music Licence, do you, at the Hand and Flower?'

'Not bloody likely.'

'So you considered the playing of a transistor a breaking of the rules? I wouldn't agree that it was, you know, providing it was done quietly and wasn't causing annoyance to other customers.'

'That's up to me, Inspector. They all know I won't stand for it.'

'Then perhaps you should have a notice saying "No Music" in both bars.'

'That's not music. It's soul-rot.'

Jean got up. 'Well, we'll see what the magistrates make of your views. Are you sure you feel all right? Anything you want?'

He said, 'Will I get my licence taken away, Inspector?'

'I can't tell you that at the moment.'

In her office she sat down with a blank note-pad before her, a habit of hers when she needed ideas to come to her, and jotted down words. Eyes. Heaviside's eyes had brought back the memory of somebody else, somebody who had sat in the Charge Room and said . . . what? Poison. Corruption. The Evil One. Stuff that sounded like temperance texts, the sort of thing one would expect to find in the Rechabite Hall. In fact, something of the kind *was* painted up there.

The Rechabite Hall. Jean put down her pencil. A light had dawned in her mind; a light by which she saw a prisoner with the eyes of a fanatic struggling between two constables, shouting out texts. Amos Baker. The man who'd found his daughter and the lodger in compromising circumstances, had beaten up both of them and his wife as well, and started throwing the furniture out on to the pavement. He was in an asylum now, certified as having gone over the edge of sanity.

She picked up the telephone and dialled the police doctor. 'If you could spare a few minutes – there's a man here I think you ought to take a look at . . .'

'George,' she said to Parrish, 'how long is it since I made a routine check on the Hand and Flower?'

He looked up the Licensed Premises file. 'Nearly a month, Ma'am.'

'Then I think it's time I made another. Tell Harry I'll want him with me.'

'Right, Ma'am.'

Regular checks on a monthly basis by the police were an accepted part of a landlord's life, welcomed by those who had no fears about being caught out violating any of the provisions of the Licensing Act. So far Jim Heaviside had a clean slate. He was not a popular landlord, but he had regulars who regarded him as one of the old school, not given to innovation or changes. There has been no reports of incidents calling for the intervention of the police – until the night when Heaviside himself caused one. He kept his books properly, was firm about the observation of permitted hours, and insisted that beer waggons should unload and deliver at a side door where they caused no obstruction to traffic.

Yet Jean said, 'I think we'll take a look round this morning, Harry.'

'Anything special, Ma'am?'

'Possibly. Just an idea.'

There was no compulsion in the Act for a member of the Force to give any particular reason for asking to inspect licensed premises. But it was unusual to arrive outside opening hours, as Jean was now doing. The door was answered by old Arnold, the only person who slept in the house other than the widower Heaviside. A potboy was washing glasses at the bar and the floor shone from the recent attentions of a cleaner, who straightened up and stared at the sight of uniforms.

Arnold looked past them at the Ford Escort. 'Haven't you brought him back, Inspector?'

'Afraid not, Arnold. Not yet.'

'I've been that worried. It were so sudden, last night . . .'

'You've never seen him like that before, then?'

'Well . . ' A secretive look came over the barman's face. 'There was one time – but it came to nowt.'

'Like to tell me? No? Well, I think we'll take a look at things.' She stepped behind the bar, followed by Newton, and opened the door faced with plate glass that led into the rear. Arnold looked shocked.

'Them's Mr Heaviside's private quarters.'

'I know. I want to see them.'

'But you never have before.'

'I am doing now.' The door led to a bare small lobby off which a cellar entrance opened; piles of crates were neatly stacked in it. Further on was a door leading to a sitting-room conventionally furnished, tidy, impersonal. Jean took in the details of it: small-screen black and white television set, a few old, cheaply-bound novels, Edgar Wallace, Rider Haggard, a cheap edition of Dickens. It might have been a room in a lodging-house, let to a different tenant every night.

At the end of a small passage were stairs. A landing at the top led to a large bedroom running the length of the building, its twin windows looking down on the street. Three-piece bedroom suite, 1930s style, dull and respectable. Jean was aware that Newton was puzzled by her interest in rooms so far from suspicious. She paused by the fireplace, and took up one by one the framed photographs on the mantelpiece. There were others on the wall: a wedding-group in which the bridegroom bore a faint resemblance to Heaviside, many years back, the same man in private's uniform of the Second World War, a christening party, a stout baby posed on a table-top, a smiling boy.

She opened the door of another room. Wherever Arnold slept, it wasn't here. There was an air of disuse about it, a scent of dust. The single bed was covered with a sheet, the outline under it uneven and lumpy. As she lifted it young Harry Newton gasped in apprehension.

'It's all right, Harry. Not a corpse.'

On the bed lay three guitars, new and beautiful, shining wood, ivory inlay, delicate strings. A shrouded shape under the window was revealed as a sort of miniature piano.

Newton said, 'He's some sort of music nut, Ma'am?'

'You could call it that. Try the wardrobe.'

The wardrobe was capacious, but it held no clothes, only a drum-kit, and some pieces of electronic equipment. Jean sighed with satisfaction.

'But what are they, Ma'am? I mean, he doesn't play them, does he?'

'No, Harry, he doesn't play them. And I should guess nobody else would ever have played them again, if we hadn't turned up.' She moved the drums aside to show him what was on the floor of the wardrobe: a hammer, a coal-chopper, a wire-cutter, an electric drill.

156

The hearing at the magistrates' court, postponed until the background to Jim Heaviside had been assembled, was somewhat different from the simple question of an assault charge. The solicitor engaged for the landlord spoke.

'Mr Heaviside became a licensee on being discharged from the Forces in 1946. He'd married during the war. In 1952 a son was born, Roger. The family were then living on the outskirts of Stockport, where Mr Heaviside managed a licensed house, the Railway Arms. The trouble seems to have begun when Roger was a teenager and became mixed up with some fairly bad types in the Manchester area. He joined some sort of pop outfit and became involved with drugs, which was when the police investigated him. Because he was basically a lad of good character Social Services tried very hard with him, but he was too badly hooked. In 1970 he died, aged eighteen, from the effects of hard-line drugs. Mr Heaviside later moved to Hartley, where his wife died shortly afterwards. I think that explains, your worships, how he came to have a fanatical hatred of the pop music he blamed in the first place for his son's death, and, however unreasonably, he decided to steal the instruments belonging to the young men whose names you already have, letting himself into the Rechabite Hall by means of an electric drill. He admits this, and planning to destroy the instruments, and any others of which he could get possession.

'A medical report will be submitted to you, indicating Mr Heaviside's mental state.'

Jean told Tom, 'They were very nice about it. Old Morris made a joke about the Devil having the best tunes and put himself in a good humour. Heaviside'll have to pay for the broken transistor, and compensate the band for the loss of admission money, and he's promised to undergo treatment.'

'Will it do any good?'

'You know more about that sort of thing than I do. There's always hope. He's pretty broken-up – it might be the turning-point.' She smiled dreamily. 'You know what I'm looking forward to? Seeing those boys' faces when they come for their instruments, and find they're all there, not a screw missing. Instead of a pile of smashed-up wood and metal.'

He touched her cheek. 'Are they having a panto at H.Q. this year? Because they've got a ready-made Fairy Godmother '

'I don't know about that. But it's nice to be right sometimes . . .'

Superintendent Hallam was going through the petty-cash book.

'Six portions cod and chips. Expensive criminals you've been entertaining, Mrs Darblay.'

'Not criminals, sir. The boys who'd had their instruments stolen from the Rechabite Hall. They seemed . . . they were very cast down, and they hadn't much money.' It sounded lame: almost everything did that she said to Hallam.

'I see. So the police are expected to feed them.' His tone was heavily sarcastic. 'After which you enter licensed premises without a warrant –'

'I didn't need one, sir.'

'– and bring about the conviction of a respected publican from whom the brewers have now withdrawn his licence.'

'That was always on the cards, once he'd been proved to have committed an offence.'

Hallam shut the petty-cash book. 'Retribution catches up with us in the end – is that what you're trying to say, Mrs Darblay? Make enough mistakes and you'll incriminate yourself? That's very true, you know. Don't forget it.'

'I'm not likely to, sir.'

Not while you're here, she added silently, and I've a nasty feeling you're here to stay.

14 A Third at Dinner

Jean tried not to take her stresses home, but it was very hard not to. Hallam made it as clear to her as if he had stated it in a memorandum that he wanted her out. He appeared, far more than was necessary, he poked and pried and criticised and tried to stir up feelings against her in her men. She guessed that at H.Q. he was doing his best to undermine the good opinion the Chief Superintendent had of her.

It was strange that Sergeant Beck, once her determined opponent, should have become her chief ally. He, too, had his reasons for disliking the new broom. Hallam's persistent efforts to enlist him and Parrish on his side had failed. He had tried cajolery, ridicule, and very subtle minor indignities, in the hope of making these two obtuse sergeants realise that they belonged under his colours, and that between them the resented female intruder could be ousted. All without effect. It was as though two lieutenants of Boudicca had refused to notice that there were Romans about.

Their skins were thick; the darts refused to stick in them. But Jean felt every one that Hallam directed at her. Her professional pride was hurt, and her feminine pride suffered as well. She had never tried to pull her sex with the lads or make the slightest capital out of it, yet here she was being treated like someone who ought to have been doing commercials for gravy cubes, with scenes of husband and kiddies arriving home out of the snow to a glowing savoury-scented kitchen. A Little Woman, scatter-brained and unforceful, the sort of woman Jean knew she was not.

Tom knew it was happening. But he had troubles of his own that made him less ready to listen to hers and support her. For over a month he had been out of work, since resigning from his Social Services job. Now Jean was the wage-earner, and he disliked it as much as he had done after the collapse of the job at Speke. They had kept separate bank accounts, and his was dwindling to the edge of overdraft.

So when she came home not her sparkling self, smiling less than she had once done, there was behind his sympathy the thought that at least she was working, not dependent on someone else. Tomorrow she would go off as usual, a day's duties before her, while he sat reading the ad. columns in all the papers or sat in a train bound for some place where a job was advertised, only too aware that his seniority of years and experience might not count against the persuasive glitter of some young executive type in a suit with a waistcoat and hair slicked across the forehead.

But the night came when he had to take notice of her as they sat down to the meal he'd prepared. The shine had gone from her hair and her skin, the lines at the corners of her long mobile mouth were more pronounced than they had ever been, and there were shadows round her eyes. As they ate and talked, he knew that she was only half with him.

'It's that bastard again, isn't it,' he said.

'Yes. Does it show? I'm sorry.'

'Don't be. It's me that ought to be sorry. I've known things weren't right and I've not done much to help.'

'You can't, love. Nobody can. It's one of those situations where irresistible force meets immovable object, and nobody wins – only the immovable object's getting a bit battered and bruised. If only he'd lay off for a bit – but he won't. Nagging women – they're a joke compared with nagging men. You know, he's wrong-footed me so often I'm beginning to wonder whether he's right about me after all.'

'It's known as eroding someone's confidence. There's a lot of it about, especially in family life. Make them feel small and they'll act small, that sort of thing.'

'Well, I don't intend to act small. He won't get that satisfaction. Only . . . well, one gets tired.'

Tom transferred himself to the only armchair in the kitchen, and beckoned. She went to him and curled up on his knee, one arm round his neck. Blackie the cat stared. The mistress had taken her usual place.

Tom asked, 'That better?'

'Mm. I don't mind being made to feel feminine by you. At least I never see "Bloody woman" written round your forehead in letters of fire . . .'

He kissed her hair. 'You won't. Jean. Got any odd leave coming to you?'

'I could rustle up about a week. Why?'

'We could go away – get you out of that maniac's path for a bit, and give me a break from job-hunting. Nowhere expensive, because you're paying, but quiet, somewhere that couldn't possibly be mistaken for Hartley.'

'That's not a bad idea. What about that place in Bowland Forest where we had that weekend? The one with the pub by the trout-stream.'

'Rathgill. Just right. I could take the new camera, and we could walk . . .'

'. . . and go and see castles and abbeys and things and just laze. It sounds like heaven. When do we leave?'

'Whenever you say.'

'I'll fix it in the morning, before Hallam can find a reason why not.'

Tom had been looking at his pocket diary. 'D'you know something? Next week's special.'

'How special?'

He grinned. 'I thought women were always supposed to remember.'

'*Tom*! Our anniversary. How rotten of me to forget – but it just shows the state of mind I'm in. Of course, that settles it. If there's any grumbling about short notice for getting a replacement, I'll produce a doctor's note. That's how desperate I am.'

But there were no noises of objection made at H.Q. It suited Hallam, indeed, that a male replacement should reign at Hartley for a week. That way, the men would find out what they'd been missing, and he would be able to collect a whole lot of ammunition against Mrs Darblay.

For Jean, the days dragged. When she finally tidied up her

office to a standard that even Hallam, with a magnifying-glass, couldn't have faulted, it seemed that several weeks had passed since she and Tom decided to go away. She told herself it was ridiculous to be so excited, when they were only going to a modest inn in a quiet spot with nothing but natural beauties to offer; but a cruise round the world would not have elated her more.

Over Saturday night a spell of dull cool weather broke, and Sunday dawned brilliantly blue and golden, a September morning at its best. As they drove north the industrial landscape fell away behind them, mills and high-rise flats and sordid terraces, and mountains came in sight, velvet green just purpling with heather, lofty fells where sheep grazed and grey stone farms nestled, rivers and streams reflecting the sky. The giant Pendle Hill was far behind them, open country before them, a tang of the sea coming over from the west.

And, quite suddenly, they were driving down the familiar lane, parallel with the clear river, towards the foursquare plain-faced inn called the Anglers' Rest. As the Mini stopped on the cobbles before it Jean felt utterly at peace, for the first time in months.

Everything at Rathgill was what they had imagined and hoped for. The mill-stream ran beneath their bedroom, built out from the back of the house, its gentle continuous murmur a better sleep-inducer than anything from a doctor's surgery, just as the piercingly fresh air went to the head more swiftly than wine. Instead of the hasty breakfast Jean prepared at home with one eye on the clock, a feast appeared every morning that could be enjoyed at leisure. Porridge perfectly made, served with cream, eggs from the inn's own hens, bacon grilled exactly as Tom liked it, local spicy sausages, home-made bread, and tea which seemed a different drink from the sort brewed in Hartley. Jean put aside all thought of her uniform; she'd worry about that when they got back home.

Standing by the parlour window, with her last cup of tea, she called Tom. 'Come and look!'

A man was walking past the inn completely surrounded by dogs. They were long-legged, straight-tailed, liver-and-white patched; their ears flopped and their noses had a sharp, alert tilt. 'Aren't they sweet!' she said. 'So disciplined-looking. They'd be a credit to our dog-handlers.'

The landlady, Mrs Birkin, who had appeared to clear the table, sniffed. 'Sweet! that's not what I'd call them, Mrs Darblay. Not when they're rampaging over t' farm-land wi' a string of great horses after 'em, doing more damage than all t' foxes in t' district wi' their tails on fire.'

'Oh, the hunt.'

'Aye. The hunt. Lord Marram believes in keeping up t' old ways, and there's plenty flattered to follow him, even them that ought to know better.'

'You're against blood-sports, Mrs Birkin?' Tom asked.

'Neither for nor against, but I'm not *for* that lot up at Marram Hall, riding roughshod over other people's land. Stone walls or fences, it's nowt to them what they smash. And talk about rogue dogs frightening the sheep – my brother had ten ewes miscarry last time hounds were his way. Took his lordship to court over it, and lost. You might know he would,' she added darkly. Picking up the loaded tray she departed.

'Doesn't like his lordship,' Jean commented. 'Prefers the foxes. I thought people who kept hens loathed foxes. You wouldn't think feelings ran so high in this peaceful part of the world, would you.'

'There's not much cap-touching around here, love.'

Discreet questioning of Mrs Birkin revealed that she was not the only person with whom Lord Marram was unpopular. He was, she said, not a real lord at all, only a jumped-up fellow who'd made a mint of money and bought his way into the title. He owned fishing rights over a long stretch of the river and was very nasty to anyone who infringed them even unknowingly. His tenants found him an ungenerous landlord, mean about repairs and maintenance. 'T' fact is,' Mrs Birkin said, 'he doesn't know how to treat country folk. He's got no business to be here at all, if you ask me. It's not as if he'd brought custom wi' him. We don't get a ha'porth of trade out of his grand friends, not we. You won't catch *them* supping ale in our bar or ringing up for a meal. No, they must go throwing their money away at the place that cousin of his runs and everybody makes such a fuss of.'

'What place is that?'

'White Harte Manor. "Best eating in the North", that's how he advertises it.' She snorted. 'Wouldn't give you tuppence for all that foreign stuff, cream and brandy and such, he cooks with, him and that turned-up-nosed wife of his.'

'The original Wicked Squire, Lord Marram, it seems,' Jean said to Tom after they had left Mrs Birkin to her hostile broodings. 'But this cousin of his ... wait a minute.' She went to their car, unlocked it, got out the Hungry Traveller's Companion, and began to leaf through it. 'White Harte Manor, Skelbeck. "Imposing Victorian High Gothic mansion ... dinners only ... chef's pâté unforgettable ... sautéed venison in juniper berries and port ... chicken smitane ... chocolate roulade à la White Harte ..." ' She shut the book. 'We're going there.'

'We are? When, and why?'

'When, for our anniversary the day after tomorrow, and why, because unlike Mrs Birkin I *would* give tuppence for something done with cream and brandy and such.'

'What's wrong with the Anglers?'

'Not a thing, it's marvellous. I just fancy something a bit more exotic for a real change, and somewhere to dress up for. I've brought the dress I wore at the Mayor's do, and I'm not going to waste it.'

Tom was looking at the entry in the Companion. 'Have you seen the prices? And that's for last year. We don't want to spend that kind of money, just for a meal.'

'Would you be saying that if you were paying? Come on, now.'

'Well ... if you wanted to go there for a treat ...'

'I do, and it doesn't matter who pays. Your turn when you've got a job. Okay?'

'If it's what you want, okay. It says here "Essential to book".'

'So we'll telephone now. From the call-box at the post

office. I've a feeling Mrs Birkin might have something to say if she heard.'

They were walking at an easy pace, Tom swinging the stick he had brought. Jean said suddenly, 'Tom.'

'Yes?'

'I've had an idea, and I'm not sure if you'll like it.'

'Try me.'

'Well . . . would you mind very much if I asked Annie to join us for the meal? I know she's lonely in that house, even though she's crazy about it, and I think she's missing Bill – you know, her Canadian. She could drive up here and stay the night at the Anglers, and go back first thing in the morning. But if you'd rather it was just you and me, I'll forget it.'

Tom took her hand. 'It's always you and me – always will be. We've had our anniversaries on our own so far, but if you want to share this one with Annie, fine. She won't feel a bit odd woman out, will she?'

'We won't let her. Thank you, love.' She laughed. 'I've just thought of something. Who was it said "After the first five years of marriage there should always be a third for dinner"?'

'Some bloody cynic or other. Never mind him.' Tom was just a shade disappointed that he was going to have to share Jean for their special evening, but he was determined not to show it. So long as it turned out well; that was all that mattered.

Annie was delighted but incredulous. 'You can't mean it. You don't want me really. You went up there to get away from Hartley.'

'You're not Hartley. And we do want you.'

The stone cottage with the wonderful views was Annie's dream of home, but it was undeniably lonely. The furniture she had bought for it was nothing like adequate, and somehow buying things just for oneself wasn't very satisfying. The job at Crossley's was absorbing during the day, but she had made no friends there yet. And she was missing Bill. It was a welcome thought that she could lock up, get into her new car, and head north to people who knew her and wanted her.

At the Anglers' Rest they were waiting, Jean glowing in a crimson dress high at the neck, clinging to the figure, her face healthy from fresh air and sun, Tom in the best suit she had made him bring. To get round the problem of drinking and driving, they hired the village taxi to take them to Skelbeck and bring them back when they telephoned. It was driven by the head of the firm, a highly competent old lady who knew the bends and twists of the lanes like the back of her hand, or possibly better.

'Here you are, Mr Darblay. White Harte Manor.'

They stared at it. Victorian High Gothic indeed, looming up against the evening sky, a conglomeration of towers and buttresses and crenellations and mock arrow-slits. Small windows with pinnacles above them stood out from the building at angles suggesting that they could not possibly have been attached to rooms, heraldic monsters glared out from coats-of-arms and electric torch-flames blazed from cressets made in Birmingham.

'Are you sure this is the right place?' Annie asked nervously.

'There's only one White Harte. Now you just ring when you want me to come for you.' Briskly old Mrs Thwaite got back into the car and in a moment was no more than two tail-lights vanishing round a corner.

'Come on,' Jean said. 'I'm looking forward to this. It may look like Pentonville, but they say the food's better.'

Inside the great arched front door an atmosphere of quiet luxury prevailed. Their feet sank into deep, scarlet carpeting, more griffins and dragons embellished the wide staircase, and the lamps were determinedly antique. A personage in immaculate evening dress, who might have sat for a portrait of the perfect butler, relieved them of their coats and whisked them silently away before returning to conduct them into a high-ceilinged drawing-room, furnished in impeccable and expensive taste. He waved them into deep chairs.

'The Colonel will be along in a moment,' he said.

Tom stared. 'What colonel?'

'Colonel Astley-Marram,' Jean said. 'Proprietor. It says so over the door.' A fair scattering of people, all prosperous-looking, sat around the room with drinks and cocktail snacks. Jean recognised them as typical manufacturers and their ladies, young executives and their elegant young wives, people who bought their clothes from the best of London, York, Harrogate. The younger women tended to wear clothes of deceptive simplicity and expensive high boots, the elder ones were not ashamed of showing off the family jewellery.

The chatter and laughter paused for the entry of a tall, brisk-moving man. He was not in evening dress, but his clothes somehow suggested that he would have found it too ordinary a uniform. He was fortyish, beginning to grey, and wore a small military-style moustache.

'The Colonel,' Jean said. 'Must be.' They watched him dart gracefully between chairs and tables, heard him greet guests. 'Lady Marten, what a pleasure. Sir Robert. Miss Felicity. Far too long since we saw you.'

'Do you suppose you *have* to be titled to come in here?' Annie murmured to Jean. 'You'd better be the Duke and Duchess of Hartley – just introduce me as the Honourable Anne.'

There was a look of slight puzzlement on the Colonel's face as he approached them. 'Good evening?' he said on a rising note.

'Good evening,' Tom replied amiably. He proffered no introductions of any kind, fictitious or otherwise.

'You *have* reserved?' The Colonel's tone suggested that it was unlikely.

'That's right. Eight o'clock.' The Colonel glanced at the handsome long-case in the corner. It showed twenty minutes to eight. Without comment he passed on. Tom looked after him. 'Sir,' he said to the retreating back. 'D'you reckon he'd have set the chucker-out on us if we'd not reserved?' he asked Jean.

'Not a doubt. I want a drink, and I'm sure you and Annie do. What about getting him back and ordering?'

'He doesn't look as if he takes orders.' They sat, increasingly less patient, for another five minutes before a waiter appeared and took their order. Soon afterwards the same grand personage who had taken their coats appeared with menus: large menus, written in violet ink on thick expensive paper. They studied them, bewildered by the enormous selection of choices. Tom glanced at the prices, and wondered if he had gone visibly pale. Wincing, he chose pâté as a starter, with *côte de veau Normande*, as a main course. Jean settled for *Coquilles St Jacques* followed by carbonnade of beef. Annie tactfully complimented her hostess with the choice of an expensive seafood pancake and the beef.

The menus were borne away and replaced by a wine list. By now Tom was quite sure he was several shades paler. Desperately, he chose the two cheapest bottles he could find, a Burgundy and a White Bordeaux. Jean was sorry for him, seeing his vain search for house wines. The wine waiter raised his eyebrows as he took the order.

'They know how to charge here,' Tom said.

'I've known worse in Vancouver,' Annie reassured him. 'Places where you weren't just glad somebody else was paying, you were deeply thankful.'

Then they waited. The hour of eight ticked over, five past, ten past. They grew increasingly impatient. Jean, her temper rising, intercepted a waiter. 'We booked a table for eight o'clock. Can we have it soon, please?'

'I'll enquire, madam.' He gave the impression that the enquiry would be less than forceful.

After another five minutes Jean stood up. 'We're going,' she announced. 'I've had about enough of this place and its bad manners. Come on.'

'But we've no car,' Tom said. 'And where would we go, anyway?'

'We can phone the taxi firm now. And we'll simply go back to the Anglers. I'm sorry about this, but I can't do with being messed about.'

As they moved towards the front door the stately waiter appeared.

'Your table is ready now, sir. If you'll come this way . . .'

Tom and Annie looked at Jean, who hesitated, then shrugged. 'All right. I suppose it'll save complications.' They followed him into a dining-room which could have doubled as a setting for *The Last of the Barons*.

The starters arrived. They looked, and tasted delicious. The spirits of the three diners began to rise. They had almost finished the course when the Colonel arrived, thunder-faced.

'I believe you have ordered the *Boeuf* and the *Veau*, sir.'

'Yes. Why, are they off?'

The Colonel disregarded this pleasantry. 'Am I to understand that you have chosen two wines from the bottom of my price-list to accompany them?'

'If you say so.'

'I do say so, sir, and I say that your taste is quite appalling. All my wines are excellent, but some are naturally more excellent than others. Perhaps you failed to realise that your chosen dishes are cooked with Calvados and Guinness respectively, and that a very, very delicately balanced choice of wine is required? Now, *this*,' he picked up the White Bordeaux from its ice-pail and looked at it contemptuously, 'might be all very well for a plain dish, possibly from my à la carte. I can't possibly permit it to be drunk with my *Veau Normande*.' He thrust it at a passing waiter. 'Take this away and bring this gentleman a *Pouilly Fumé Les Griottes '78*.'

'But we've had a glass with our starters,' Tom protested, 'and it was . . .'

'And with the *Boeuf*,' the Colonel went on relentlessly, 'a particularly special *'66 St Emilion*. I'll have it sent up.' He strode away before anybody could say anything.

'This place,' Jean said with restrained fury, 'is a clip-joint. I wish we could get out now without making a scene, but we can't, and I don't want to ruin the evening completely. I knew we ought to have gone before.'

'Jean,' Annie said, 'it's going to be shockingly expensive. Please will you let me help out?'

'That's very kind, Annie, but no. I'll do the paying, or rather Tom will with my cheque book, and then I'll do some investigating into the Colonel and his restaurant. I've got a strong feeling he's a villain, and it'll give me very great pleasure to prove it.'

The main course arrived, and the replacements for the

wines, borne by an expressionless waiter. Without much appetite now, they got through it. Tom rather disliked his veal. Jean said the beef was all right. 'But I expect I could have done it like this myself, given time. At least it's tender.'

'Yes . . .' Annie said.

The wine may have been superb, but it was soured for the drinkers. 'If the beef's cooked with Guinness, why not drink Guinness with it?' Jean asked. 'It would be a lot cheaper, even if you ordered it by the quart. I don't know about you two, but I don't want anything else. Just the bill.'

When the bill was placed before Tom he looked at it for moments, silently. One of the wines was £9.50, the other £15, on top of extortionate prices for the food, a heavy cover charge, and Service Not Included. Without consulting Jean he added no service tip. The waiter's face registered disgust and disapproval. Nobody said good night as they left. The Colonel wasn't there to say it. Tom telephoned the taxi firm; by silent agreement they waited outside in the fresh air.

Annie broke the silence. 'He was doing it to other people. I heard him two tables away, criticising someone, when he was going the rounds.'

'I don't care if he was criticising the Archbishop of York and the Lord Lieutenant,' Jean said. 'He probably knows them, and he didn't know us – that was why he behaved so unspeakably. They're strangers, heave a brick at 'em, that's his motto. Among others.'

At the Anglers' Rest Mrs Birkin was waiting up. 'So you're back,' she said. 'Oh, I know where you've been, Mrs Thwaite let it out. Did you enjoy yourselves?'

Jean said 'No. Can we have some brandies, please, Mrs Birkin – large ones?'

The landlady brought a bottle and three glasses to the table in the bar. 'Pour for yourselves. I can trust you.'

'Who is this guy, the Colonel?' Tom asked. 'Is he a real Colonel, for instance?'

'I don't know about Colonel, but he were in t' Guards as a young man. Then he took a fancy to the restaurant business and trained for it abroad. He got White Harte Manor cheap, through his lordship, and started building up business same way, getting his lordship's pals to come and spread the word.'

'Old Boys' League.'

'If that's what they call it. *I'd* call it taking trade away from folk that's been here for generations. He can afford to do it, you see, because he gets his food cheap from Marram Hall – fish and game, and that. Gets his staff cheap, too, unemployment being what it is, and pays minimum wages, so I've heard.'

'What a lovely feller,' Annie said. 'I don't think I've ever heard such rudeness, anywhere.'

'Oh, they like that, some folk. Well, don't say I didn't warn you. I wish I'd said more, only I never thought you'd be daft enough to go there. I only hope you'll tell others when you get back to Hartley.'

'Don't worry, we will.'

'Good night, then.'

Sipping brandy, Jean began to feel the exasperations of the evening simmering down. 'I'm sorry, both of you. It was my fault that we went to the wretched place, and Mrs Birkin's quite right about it being daft of me. I meant it for a treat, but it didn't turn out like that. I only wish I could do something about it. What, though? It may be offensive to force an expensive wine on a customer instead of a cheap one, but it's not breaking the law. We weren't pleased with the service, and if we'd been tough we could have refused to pay part of the bill. But my feeling is that the Colonel would have made the sort of scene I wasn't prepared to face.'

'Could you have made it a police matter?' Annie asked.

'No – it's purely civil. Even if I'd been in uniform, there was nothing I could do, officially. Only if the meal hadn't been what the menu described it as . . .'

Annie was swirling the brandy round and round in her glass, thinking. Outside a wind had got up, buffeting gently against the old building. 'Jean,' she said at last.

'Yes?'

'I've been wondering whether I ought to say this – you'll see why. But I think, taking it all round, I should.'

'I'm listening.'

171

'Well. You said the beef was tender, didn't you?'

'Yes – beautifully. Wasn't yours?'

'Perfect. Only . . . it wasn't beef.'

Two pairs of eyes were fixed on her. 'Go on,' Jean said.

'It was horse.'

'*What*?'

'I know, you see, because I've had it in Canada. You know the French don't mind about things like that, and it's far cheaper than beef. The first time I had it was with a French-Canadian guy who thought I was mad when I made a fuss. It cropped up occasionally after that, and I got to ignore it, though I tried to pick other things off the menu which couldn't possibly be that. So I can't mistake it now – even done in Guinness. I'm sorry – I didn't want to tell you.'

Jean poured another brandy for Tom, seeing him shudder. 'Are you all right, love? I'm glad you did tell me, Annie. I've got him now, I think. The Food and Drugs Act makes it a criminal offence to serve food which isn't what it says it is. Tomorrow we'll look up the local Environmental Health Inspector – and while he's there he can have a glance round the kitchens. Oh, I shall enjoy this!'

'But how d'you think he does it?' Annie asked. 'I mean, in France you can buy horse-meat openly at – I think they're called charcuteries chevaleries, there's a horse's head over the door – but not here. So, how?'

Tom said, 'What about the hunt?'

'Of course! This Lord Marram – one of his horses breaks a leg or gets past hunting, so he sells it to his cousin.'

Jean said, "He gets his stuff cheap from Marram Hall." Not only fish and game. Well, we'll sort him out. Come on, time for bed.'

'I'm going to dash off in the morning, if you don't mind,' Annie said. 'I've got a meeting at ten and I don't want to be late. So I won't see you. But thank you so much for asking me to share your evening – I enjoyed it, really I did, in spite of everything.' She kissed them both. 'And don't worry about the, er, main course. It can't hurt you.'

She watched them wistfully as they went up the narrow

staircase together. Jean was saying to Tom, 'I never said Happy Anniversary to you. That was what it was all about.'

'Never mind. Say it now.'

The Environmental Health Inspector was deeply interested to hear about the cuisine at White Harte Manor. He looked at his appointments and decided he could spare time to go out there in the late morning. Highly respectful to Jean on hearing of her status, he suggested that she and Tom might like to accompany him.

'Thanks, but you don't want too many people under your feet. We'll come for the ride and wait for you.'

From the car they watched him go in, brief-case in hand. For almost an hour they strolled in the grounds before he came out again. The Colonel was with him, looking agitated and talking a great deal. At the door the Inspector shook his head repeatedly. Finally he broke away and returned to them at the car. Jean half-expected to see the Colonel raise a shotgun and pick him off.

The Inspector was smiling. 'You were quite right. Part of a horse carcass in the refrigerator – I've got samples. Also bad hygienic conditions in kitchens and staff washrooms. Mr Astley-Marram admitted that his supplies came from Marram Hall, so that's my next port of call. Like to come with me?'

'No, thanks, we'll confine ourselves to a report to the Hungry Traveller's Companion.'

They drove back to the Anglers' Rest through moor and glen and forest stretches, in weather veering from sudden rain to flashing sunshine. There at the inn lunch was waiting, fresh river trout, apple pie and cheese. They ate it looking across to where shadows chased across the broad side of Rath Fell. A red squirrel darted down a tree a few yards away from the inn, gave them a comprehensive view of itself as it ate a nut, then vanished like a spirit. The Birkins' huge black and white dog lay on the floor by the Darblays' feet, fixing them sometimes with a thoughtful brown eye, then sleeping again, as though it hadn't a care in the world, which was probably the case.

And Jean knew that she was enjoying herself more than she had done for years, and that she was beginning to dread going back. The events of the night before reflected her own situation, she thought: for a short time Colonel Astley-Marram had seemed a bogey-man figure, an instrument of public humiliation and blatant fraud, but she had set the law of the country on him and proved him no more than a thing of straw. In Hartley there waited for her one who was a true bogey, who hated her and wished her ill. Even he was working against her, undermining her authority, preparing the day when she would have no choice but to leave the job she loved, and go – where?

Tom said, 'Hey, come back. You were miles away, did you know?'

She managed to smile. 'Yes, I know. But I'm back now. Here, with you, for the rest of the time we've got.'